Revelation

of the Elite

Book 2 in the series

A compilation of personal log entries, interviews, stories, and memories by

J.C. Stevens

For my incredible wife Janet and my adorable daughters, Alana and Ashlynn. You are each so gifted and talented. You are the elite in my world.

Acknowledgements

Thank you to my advanced readers who acted as editors, spell checkers, comma police, and my support group.

To Janet Dapper, Alana Dapper, Ashlynn Dapper, Velma Hamon, Matt Reif and Christina Reif - your support in crafting this story is appreciated more than you know. Thank you for your honest feedback and consistent encouragement.

To my graphic design artist, germancreative, thank you for intuitively seeing the vision in my head and making it a reality.

Prologue

For as long as I can remember, I pursued everything that was meaningless. For more than forty years I chased power, prestige, and importance. My efforts led me to be the best monitor in U.S history. I rose above the hardships, made my own way, and conquered misfortune. I sacrificed everything I had. I even sacrificed things that didn't belong to me to feed my ego and self-indulgences. That was who I was—a worthless man who deserved nothing less than a painful, lonely death. But instead of reaping the full consequences of my unethical behavior, I found something amazing sitting in a mud puddle in my backyard. I found redemption.

That day, I was confronted with my own wickedness. Jacob Monroe had both the right and the capability to end my life, but he instead opened my eyes to who I really was. When he spared my life and walked away, I was left with the emptiness of chasing the wind and the regret of selfish ambition.

I deeply regret the things I've done and the people I've hurt, but I will never regret that day. I was ready and willing to die. I deserved it. But it was in that moment that I heard a voice and experienced a feeling that changed my life forever. I experienced both the peace and the awesome power of the God that Jacob and Robert knew—the God I had resisted and denied for most of my life.

In that moment, everything changed for me. On that cold, soggy, and dirty day, I embarked on a journey to intentional relationships that I had never known before. That moment represented a revelation of a new life I didn't know existed. It was the start of a new era in my life. It birthed a time when my perspective changed and secrets long hidden were revealed.

Tom Marshall

Former Senior Lead Monitor – United States Government

Chapter 1

The black of night and a rainy mist engulfed the PMC Atlanta Children's Hospital as a mysterious figure walked toward the front entrance. He was short in stature with dirt-stained jeans and a black hooded jacket that shielded any recognizable characteristics from the hospital security cameras.

He shuffled by the front desk, glancing up just long enough for the receptionist to recognize his face. He continued walking as she spoke.

"Hey, what are you doing here so late? Are you okay?"

He didn't respond. His focus was fixed on the path ahead of him as he made his way to the south stairwell. She didn't see the pain in his eyes or the despair on his face. She also didn't see him as a threat, so she dismissed their brief interaction and shifted her focus back to her paperwork.

He moved steadily up the stairs with his hands shoved in his jacket pockets and his eyes downward toward his feet, watching every step. The first floor of the hospital was primarily administration offices, the cafeteria, and the gift shop. The second floor was dedicated entirely to research. The lab staff studied some of the most significant and common ailments seen in the hospital in hopes of developing cures to eradicate diseases. The third, fourth, and fifth floors of the hospital were home to children with terminal illnesses.

He emerged from the stairwell on the third floor. The walls were covered with brightly painted murals, and the floors were shiny. The halls smelled clean and sounded quiet except for the small hums of the air conditioning and filtration systems.

As the door to the stairwell closed behind him, the mysterious figure walked toward room 301 and slowly entered. The room was dark and sterile. In the hospital bed next to the window, a six-year-old girl named Alicia was sleeping peacefully. Her skin was pale, and her head was bald. There were several small tubes and wires attached to her frail, little body, but she had grown so accustomed to them that it didn't interrupt her sleep. He quietly approached and stood at the side of her bed. He stared at her for a moment.

Without making a sound, he reached out and placed his fingertips on her arm. Alicia didn't move. He carefully grasped her forearm in his hand and stood motionless. He remained by her side for only a few minutes before removing his hand and turning to slip out the door as quietly as he had arrived.

He seemed to know the layout of the floor and the routine of the nursing staff well enough to evade their detection. He repeated this pattern in every occupied room on the third floor. In each room he only stayed a few minutes.

He entered the north stairwell and began to climb to the fourth floor of the hospital, but he ascended at a much slower pace. His legs felt heavy, and he was almost staggering as he walked. Before walking through the door to the fourth floor, he removed his hooded jacket and left it in the stairwell. His face was pale and sweaty. He quietly slipped into every occupied room on the fourth floor, just as he had done on the third floor.

Jack was a long-term resident of room 412. He was fourteen years old and had been in and out of the hospital so many times that he lost count. As much as he had become accustomed to the sounds and smells of the hospital, Jack was a very light sleeper. When the door to his room opened, it startled him from his slumber. He sat up halfway and gasped when he saw someone closing the door and walking toward his bed.

"Shhh. It's okay, Jack."

"What time is it? Why are you here so late? Is your mom here?" Jack rattled off questions in a groggy voice, still disoriented from the sudden awakening.

"Lay back down, Jack. Everything is going to be okay. Everything is going to be even better than okay," the voice whispered.

Jack complied with the request but still asked questions that remained unanswered.

"You don't look so good. Are you sick? You know you can't be here if you're sick. It will put too many of us at risk. Why aren't you talking to me?"

There was no reply. Jack felt a warm touch on his leg. It was soothing and different than anything he had ever experienced. He leaned his head back on the pillow as if he were soaking in the warmth, and he became so calm that he drifted back off to sleep.

The visitor released his hold on Jack and staggered to the door. He became weaker and slower after visiting each room on the floor. His body felt heavier than he could handle as he finished the last room on the fourth floor. He then made his way back to the stairwell.

He trudged up the stairs, colder and weaker than he had ever been in his life. His body was dragging up each step, and his breathing was erratic. He held tight to the handrail but could no longer hold himself up. Overcome by weakness, he fell to the ground. His body slumped over along the wall of the steps.

Hours later, the cold winter rain vanished. The warm sunlight broke through the windows of the PMC Atlanta Children's Hospital. On a typical day, the hope of sunlight faded into a solemn atmosphere in the daily routine of tests and treatments. The typical day quickly evolved into a historic day.

4

Throughout the normally quiet halls of the third and fourth floor, new sounds were heard. Sounds of children laughing, singing, and playing filled the building. Doctors and nurses flooded the area to make sense of it all. The hospital laboratory staff was overwhelmed with requests for tests to validate what the children already knew. They were healed—completely.

There was no reasonable explanation for the miracle that happened that night. The joy of what they found that morning was tainted only by what they found in the stairwell between the fourth and fifth floors. The cold, limp body of a young man the hospital staff knew and loved lay lifeless on the stairs.

Chapter 2

Tom Marshall Personal Log File BPRV2813

I sat in the mud puddle for a what felt like hours. I was afraid that if I moved, the breeze would stop blowing on my face. I feared the peace would leave as suddenly as it had appeared. I was emotionally torn. I begged God to forgive me and embraced the spiritual force that I had denied for my entire life. The change was startling and overwhelming.

The rain stopped, and a break in the clouds developed enough to let a few rays of sunlight dance around me. I mustered up the courage to stand but kept my eyes closed for a few moments to let the feeling linger. I walked to my rear porch with rainwater still dripping from my hair and clothes. I was soaked in mud and filthy from head to toe. I glanced around to make sure my neighbors were not watching and undressed as much as decently possible, leaving my nasty clothes on the same chair that had caused me to stumble to the ground. I walked briskly to the shower and scrubbed every inch of my mud-stained body. I had never felt so clean.

After my shower, I dressed and called George. Still keeping business first, I cancelled our meeting that was scheduled for the afternoon. Somewhat reluctantly, I then told George everything that had happened. I kept him on the phone for thirty minutes confessing my actions and recanting the confrontation with Jacob. I fully expected George to think I was crazy when I told him what I heard and felt after Jacob left, but instead he acknowledged it as if the situation was more familiar than strange. The confession was difficult at first but got easier as I kept talking.

George and I had a unique situation to deal with. Many of the actions I had taken were criminal and punishable by law. For the first time in my life, I was willing to own up to my deeds and pay the consequences for all the damage I had done. Unfortunately, it wasn't that easy. I couldn't just surrender myself to the authorities without risking full disclosure of the elite, the monitoring department, and all the information I was sworn to keep secret.

After a lengthy discussion without a real solution, I forced the burden of decision on George and committed to yield to whatever action he thought was appropriate. His only request is that I not put the program at risk by divulging any information to anyone just yet. I was still loyal to the mission of the monitoring department, so I gave my word with one small stipulation. I asked George for permission to talk to the Monroe family. He agreed.

In typical fashion, George asked that I give him the rest of the week to consider the next reasonable course of action. I conceded to take a few days off to give George some time to think. It also would give me some time to really comprehend what had happened, in addition to doing some necessary home repair work on my front door.

I barricaded my front entry way as much as physically possible until the morning. I awoke bright and early feeling a mixture of emotions that ranged from fear to peace. Once I was dressed, I left to purchase a new front door, some hardware, tools, and paint. While driving to the home improvement store, I heard the news about the miraculous events at the PMC Atlanta Children's Hospital and immediately called George. He admitted that he was aware of the event and was checking into it. Considering the circumstances, he re-emphasized the importance of keeping everything, including my previous actions, confidential.

As I finished installing my new front door that evening, I suddenly felt a heavy conviction. The Monroe family came to mind, and the heaviness of my guilt made my heart ache. It was as clear to me as if someone had told me directly to my face. I had to visit them and attempt to make things right.

After a restless night, I woke the next morning with a lingering pit in my stomach. I got dressed and prepared to drive to Griffin, Georgia. I spent the entire morning trying to piece together the words in my head. I didn't know what to say or how to say it. I couldn't even think of facing Jacob, not without a plan. I stopped three separate times to turn my car around. I wanted to abandon the crazy notion of interacting with the family I had hurt so deeply, but each time the conviction overpowered my cowardice.

I had no idea what I would face. Did Jacob tell Robert, Suzanna, and Christina about what happened? How would they react?

The questions fueled my fear, but I knew I wouldn't be able to live with myself if I didn't try to make things right. When I was only twenty minutes from Robert's house, I called him from my cell phone.

"Hello."

"Robert. Hi, it's Tom."

"Good morning, Tom, what can I do for you?"

We were off to a good start. From the tone of his voice and his response to my call, I concluded that Robert didn't know.

"Robert, I need to talk to you and Suzanna face-to-face. Do you mind if I come over in a few minutes?"

"Sure, Tom. We don't have much planned for today. Is everything alright?"

Well, that was a loaded question. Not knowing exactly how to answer, I decided instead to end the call abruptly and save the remainder of the conversation for a face-to-face discussion.

"Yes, Robert. We just need to talk. I'll see you soon."

Tom Marshall Personal Log File BPRV2813
End of Record

Chapter 3

Tom's car moved slowly up the driveway to the Monroe house and came to a stop in front of their porch. He shut off the engine and tilted his head back with his eyes closed. He was still uncertain of what to say, but the conviction of his heart compelled him toward the inevitable conversation.

Suzanna appeared from the front door and walked to the edge of the porch railing. Her flour-stained apron was a clear indication that there had been some baking going on. As Tom approached the front door, the smell of fresh cookies reminded him of his last visit when he tried to trick Jacob into helping stop Richard. The shameful memory made the short walk to the door emotionally painful. Despite Tom's internal struggle, her eyes met his, and her smile was warm and inviting.

"Good morning, Mrs. Monroe." Suddenly his apprehension was not as strong, and he began to feel more comfortable as he climbed the steps to the porch. Suzanna maintained her southern hospitality and welcomed him with a hug before inviting him in the house. Robert was seated in the living room waiting for his arrival. He stood to shake Tom's hand as he walked in, and then invited him to sit down. Suzanna sat down next to Robert and reached for his hand.

"Thank you, Robert, for allowing me to stop by on short notice."

"Certainly, Tom. You're always welcome."

Tom was still a bit uncomfortable with small talk, so he jumped right to the purpose of his visit.

"Robert, I have a confession to make, and I'm not sure how to handle it." Tom's rehearsed speech left him, and his mind went blank. Robert leaned forward a little and locked his eyes on Tom's face. This made him feel a little intimidated, but he knew there was no escaping the confession.

"Well, Tom, no need for formalities. We like straight and honest talk here, even if the news isn't so good. It's probably best to just go ahead and spit it out."

A heavy sigh crossed his lips, and he continued, "Robert. Suzanna. I have done something terrible, and my actions have caused your family a lot of pain. More pain than you even realize." Tom hung his head and stared at a spot on the hardwood floor. He couldn't bear to look at their faces as he continued his confession.

"What your family has gone through recently...I'm so sorry...It was my fault."

Robert leaned back in his seat with a perplexed look on his face as Tom continued.

"I caused the accident that shattered Jacob's chip, paralyzed Christina, and took away their child. I didn't know they were pregnant, and I didn't mean for anyone to get hurt. I was desperate to release Jacob from his restrainer chip so I could use him to help capture Richard. It was wrong. It was very wrong and so selfish. I didn't see it then, but I see it now. I am so sorry."

Both Robert and Suzanna sat motionless. As Tom spoke the words, they seemed shocking even to himself. He could only imagine what they were thinking. Robert's forehead was crinkled, and his eyebrows furrowed as he tried to absorb the information. He didn't say a word, so Tom continued.

"After the fight downtown, I thought my scheme had worked and everything was going to be okay, but it wasn't. Jacob found out about my plan, and he confronted me. He was so angry. I thought he was going to kill me. At the time, there was a part of me that wanted him to. I felt so terrible and guilty. Instead of giving me what I deserved, he left me sitting cold and wet in a mud puddle in my back yard. He just turned away and left without laying a finger on me. It was then and there that I realized just how wretched I was. I cried out to God and experienced something that I just can't explain. I know that I am a different man now, and I want to do the right thing. I need to make things right with you and your family, but I don't know how. I don't even know if that is possible."

Tom suddenly realized that as he was rambling and paused to look up at their faces. He expected to see anger, but instead saw brokenness. Suzanna was crying, and Robert's face was full of compassion. Tom's voice crackled as one last question escaped his lips.

"How do you forgive the unforgivable?"

Robert closed his eyes for a moment to compile his response. He silently prayed for God to give him the words to say and the strength to say them. Suzanna sat quietly, wiping the tears from her face. She held Robert's hand tight as he took a long breath. His face relaxed as he looked Tom in the eyes.

"Tom, what you did was wrong. You caused a lot of pain to a lot of people. You will need to carry part of that burden for the rest of your life. It's not easy to accept it, but it's certainly not unforgivable. You can imagine this is all surprising for us to hear, and it's going to take some time for it to really sink in."

Tom was shocked. Robert's response was what he had hoped for, but not what he expected.

"Robert, will you please forgive me for what I have done?"

Without hesitation he responded with a nod and said, "Yes, Tom, we forgive you."

"Thank you both. I can't image how shocking and painful this is to both of you. I…"

"Tom," Robert said interrupting as he sat motionless still holding Suzanna's hand, "you really don't need to start another apology. Unless there's something else you need to confess."

"Well, no, there's nothing else, but I know that I'm not done. I need to talk to Jacob and Christina."

"Of course, Tom. Why don't you join us for lunch this coming Sunday? I think that will be the best time to talk. It will give everyone some time to calm down and think through all this."

"That would be great," Tom responded.

"You can meet us at First Baptist Church on Sunday morning. The service starts at ten. After church, we will all meet up here at our house for some of the best southern cooking in all of Georgia," he said glancing at Suzanna's face to ensure she received the compliment.

Realizing that he had just been duped into going to church, Tom smiled and nodded.

"Thank you again, Robert. I will see you this weekend."

As Robert stood, Suzanna jumped up as if awaking from a daze and exclaimed, "Oh my, the cookies. I'm sorry Tom, I forgot to offer you…"

"It's quite alright, Mrs. Monroe."

"No, no, let me give you some for the road," she said as she scurried into the kitchen. She was still processing all that Tom had confessed. She didn't know how to handle the shocking information, so she fell back into her default hospitality mode. She caught him just as he followed Robert out the front door and handed him a bag of warm cookies.

They parted cordially, though Robert and Suzanna were still in shock. The knot in Tom's stomach held fast as he drove home fixated on what he would say to Jacob.

Chapter 4

Tom's alarm sounded early Sunday morning as the sun broke through the curtains in his bedroom, striking him directly in the face. He bypassed his normal routine of hitting the snooze button and rolled out of bed with some fear about talking with Jacob. There were so many questions swirling in his head. Would Jacob be as gracious as Robert had been? Would he still be angry? If he were still angry, would he show the same restraint as he did before?

Tom soon realized that he could spend all his energy asking questions that he didn't have answers to. At the very least, he was relieved that Robert had suggested a group setting for his conversation with Jacob. It would be somewhat awkward to beg for forgiveness in front of everyone there, but there was less likelihood that Jacob would end his life in the midst of a family gathering.

Tom was proud of himself for arriving at the church ten minutes early. He was pleased to see that they had guest parking spots near the front of the building but disappointed to see that the entire guest parking area was full. It made him wonder if they really had that many guests every Sunday. Ultimately, he found a parking spot farther out and realized that ten minutes early was not early enough.

Suzanna greeted him at the door with a smile on her face and escorted him to their seats. Tom sat at the end of the aisle next to Robert. Suzanna took her seat next to her husband with Christina and Jacob on the other end of the row. The aisleway was wide enough for Christina's wheelchair to park without blocking the walkway. Tom made brief eye contact with both Jacob and Christina. The church service had just begun so there wasn't any time for a formal greeting or handshake. Jacob's facial expression was difficult to read, so Tom was still uncertain how lunch would turn out.

Tom enjoyed the church service but was anxious to get back to the Monroe house to settle things with Jacob. He followed Robert and Suzanna back to their house and sat in the living room with Robert while Suzanna attended to lunch preparations. Jacob and Christina arrived a few minutes later. They required more time to transition while working around Christina's wheelchair. Almost as if she timed it perfectly, Suzanna had lunch on the table just as Jacob wheeled his wife through the front door.

They all sat at the table and endured an awkward silence after Robert blessed the meal. Everyone knew they had to talk about what happened, but no one wanted to initiate the conversation. Jacob and Tom exchanged some brief glances but never maintained eye contact for more than a moment at a time. After thinking about it too long, Tom felt it was his responsibility to break the ice.

"Jacob, Christina, I came here because I needed to apologize for what I did to both of you."

For the first time since they sat down, Jacob's eyes locked onto Tom's face. Jacob's expression was torn as if part of him wanted to kill Tom and part of him wanted to just understand everything that had happened. Christina reached up and rested her hand on his arm as a gesture of encouragement.

"Dad told me why you wanted to talk, Mr. Marshall." Jacob seemed at a loss for words. He knew what he wanted to say, but the words were not flowing quite like he had expected.

Tom continued, "That day you came over and confronted me…it changed my life. I never meant for anybody to get hurt. I'm here today to tell you how sorry I am. I need to ask you to forgive me, but I understand if you won't."

Jacob paused.

"Mr. Marshall, I want to…and I know that I should forgive you, but to be honest, it's going to take some time. You took away almost everything that means so much to me. The thought of what you did to my family made me so angry. It became a rage inside of me that I have never felt before. Every time I see my beautiful wife trapped in this wheelchair…"

Jacob stopped. Tears welled up in his eyes, and he broke his focus on Tom as he looked down at his plate. He wasn't going to finish that statement. He didn't have to. The pain and the internal conflict were evident.

Christina was feeling the anguish too. She knew that she had to be strong and stable for Jacob. She gently rubbed his arm as the tears flowed quietly down her face. Her bottom lip quivered. She hated seeing Jacob struggle with his emotions. They had talked so many times about the accident. They spent countless nights grieving the loss of their first child. She still had occasional nightmares that brought back the feelings of helplessness as their car flipped repeatedly down the road. The conversation had stirred so many emotional memories, but Christina resolved herself to stay strong for Jacob. The long pause was broken by Tom's response.

"I understand, Jacob." Tom continued, "I will do whatever it takes to make it up to you."

Everyone felt tense as an awkward silence filled the dining room. Christina kept her focus on Jacob as he struggled to compose his response. She knew he was holding his emotions inside. He wanted to do what was right, but he felt the need to be guarded with the man who brought so much pain to his life.

22

"Whatever it takes?" Jacob asked repeating Tom's sentiment.

"Yes. Anything."

Jacob had given a lot of thought to what he would say in this moment. He recalled the list of requests he planned to ask Tom to fulfill. He pulled his focus back to Tom's face.

"First, promise me that you'll never put my family in danger again."

"That one is easy. I promise, Jacob, I'll never put your family in danger again."

"Second, promise me that you'll never ask or manipulate me to use my strength."

"I think that's more than fair. You have my word. What else can I do?"

"Tom," Robert said, "Jacob and I talked about what he needed from you to regain his trust. We agreed that these two requests represented a reasonable effort to put us on a path of reconciliation. We also agreed that although you do need to earn our trust, you shouldn't need to earn our forgiveness. We forgive as we are forgiven with no conditions attached."

Tom nodded as Robert continued.

"We would like you to join us for church and lunch again next week."

"Sure, if that is okay with Jacob."

Jacob looked at Christina and they both nodded in agreement. Not wanting to carry the apology discussion any further and risk upsetting Jacob, Tom opted to change the subject.

"Has George contacted you yet to schedule another restrainer chip implant?"

"No," replied Robert, "He said as long as we weren't seeing any side effects, we can take our time. Jacob is learning to manage his strength and we're keeping a close eye on him to make sure nothing else is changing."

"What happens if I decide not to get another restrainer chip?" Jacob asked, not directing the question at anyone in particular.

Jacob's statement seemed to startle everyone at the table. They all stopped eating and focused their attention on him. The change in subject helped him regain his composure, and he spoke as if he had carefully thought through his words. Christina was the only person at the table who didn't have a surprised look on her face. She kept her hand on his arm as he continued.

"We're just not sure it's the right thing to do. The strength is helpful with taking care of the farm and my wife." Jacob looked back down at his plate and began moving some of the peas around with his fork. He then looked up and directed his next question at Robert.

"What do you think God wants me to do, Dad?"

"I don't know, son, but I am sure that He will show you in due time."

Suddenly, Tom felt like an outsider intruding on an intimate family discussion. It was awkward for him to sit and spectate, but it would have been more awkward to leave. As if watching a game of tennis, Suzanna, Christina, and Tom shifted their heads back and forth as they listened to the conversation between Robert and Jacob. No one dared to interrupt.

"Was it a mistake that I was born with this? Is there a purpose for it?" Jacob asked.

These were all very difficult questions that Jacob had been struggling with. Tom leaned forward as if he were striving to be the first to hear the words that came from Robert's mouth.

"I don't know all the answers to your questions, son. What I do know is that God doesn't make mistakes. He knew you were going to have this ability just like He knew that your sister would have abilities that we can't explain. I do believe God orchestrates the things in our life, but we mustn't confuse that with blaming God for the bad things. I know it's hard son; it's been hard on all of us. I believe that God only trusts the hard times with those who are strong in faith, not to break us but to make us even stronger. Our job is not to figure it out, but to trust."

"So, if God orchestrated this, then what should I do with it?"

"Before she died, Julie healed a lot of people. After she was gone, your mom and I struggled with the purpose for her death. We wondered why God would allow someone who could help so many people be taken so soon. We thought she could have helped so many more people if she had lived longer."

"That makes a lot of sense, Dad."

"It did until we realized something. God doesn't need to use us at all. If God wants to heal someone, He will. He doesn't need to work through us, but He chooses to. That is the great part of life, that we can be used by God to do great things.

"So, do you think God wants to use me?" Jacob asked.

Tom sat silently and watched the conversation unfold. In his mind, he was asking the same question about himself. Robert looked his son in the eyes and smiled.

"Indeed, I do, son. I respect the fact that you don't want to feel used by men for what you can do, but I believe that doesn't mean that you shouldn't be used at all."

Robert's response left everyone speechless. Jacob was mentally processing the conversation. Nothing further was said about the chip or Tom's confession through the rest of lunch. After dealing with some heavy topics, everyone understood that the rest of the conversation should be left to small talk.

Jacob and Christina left shortly after the meal. Tom opted to linger, hoping for some more dialog with Robert. His wish was granted as Robert invited him to sit on the front porch for some after-lunch coffee.

"Seems like there's a lot on your mind, Tom."

"It's painfully obvious, isn't it?"

Robert grinned.

"I just don't understand it. I don't understand any of it. I don't understand what happened to me that day in my back yard. I don't understand your reaction when you found out that the car accident was my fault. I don't understand how you, Jacob, Christina, or anybody else could choose to forgive. It all just seems unreal."

"Grace is experiential but not explainable," Robert said, still grinning. Tom had no idea what that meant, and his facial expression screamed for Robert to say more.

"Tom, you're a smart guy. You want to be able to explain everything. There are some things, in fact, the most important things in life, that you can't explain. You just have to experience them."

Tom was trying to understand, but the words seemed so overwhelming.

"Have you ever known anyone who was blind?" Robert asked.

"Yes."

"How would you explain light to a blind person?"

Tom remained silent. His brain made several attempts to formulate an answer, but no rational answer was evident.

"Tom, you can't explain light. Your best attempt wouldn't even come close. You also can't explain grace. To fully understand grace, forgiveness, and love, you must experience them. The more you experience them, the more you understand them. That's just the way life works. For the longest time, Suzanna and I couldn't understand why God took Julie at such a young age. Looking back on it now, even though we still don't fully understand it, we know that we are stronger because of it. I see you wrestling with understanding grace, and I see Jacob wrestling with understanding his purpose. I don't have the answers to all the 'why' questions, but I do know that situations like this are not accidents. They are meant to be experienced so that we can better understand."

Tom listened carefully wishing he had written those thoughts down or that he had recorded their conversation. His mind was overwhelmed with absorbing all that Robert had told him.

"Thank you, Robert. That's quite a lot to process."

"I hope it helps, Tom."

"I am sure it will. Thank you again for lunch."

After their conversation, Tom committed to returning the next Sunday and politely excused himself. Robert's words echoed through his head for the entire drive home. There was great wisdom in what Robert said, and Tom's level of respect for Robert Monroe hit an all-time high. Taking the first steps to make things right with the Monroe family relieved a lot of anxiety in his life. Tom only hoped that his meeting with George the next morning would go as smoothly.

Chapter 5

Even after the serenity that Tom felt following his visit with the Monroe family, he didn't get a lot of sleep. His mind kept racing through scenarios. Ironically, the same skill that allowed Tom to predict every possible scenario and made him effective as a monitor was the very thing keeping him up most of the night. He finally fell asleep two hours before the alarm woke him up again. It was time to go to work, face George, and accept whatever fate was waiting for him.

The old office building was quiet and dusty from the lack of activity over the past few months. The only rooms that had not been totally neglected for months were the ones used as a tactical operations center when the team was tracking Richard. It had only been a few weeks since the incident with Richard, but for Tom, it felt like years.

George was already in his old office when Tom arrived. He paused near the entrance at the end of the hallway not knowing if he should go to George's office or to the room that used to be his own office.

"Good morning, Tom," George said as he popped out from his office door.

"Good morning, George. I assume we need to talk."

"Yes, we do. Please meet me in the conference room. I'll be there in just a minute."

Tom followed his instructions and walked to the conference room. Out of habit, he sat in the same chair he always occupied during group meetings. George came in just moments after Tom sat down with a notepad, pen, and a few files in his hand.

"Do you have any good news for me, George?"

"There's always some good news, my friend. For starters, you're not going to jail."

"That is a relief. How much influence did you have over that?"
"Quite a bit, actually."

"Well then, I owe you at least a 'thank you'".

George smiled. Tom's demeanor and responses seemed different than what George was used to. The overconfident Tom with a flare of arrogance had been replaced with a man who had been broken and humbled. George took a mental note of the change, but he thought it was best to continue with the business discussion.

"Without going into detail, I reviewed the case with some of the internal affairs guys at the Bureau and with Greg Bradshaw."

"Greg Bradshaw?"

"Yes, he is upper management level at the Bureau. Although we agreed not to pursue any legal course of action for what happened, you don't have a job here anymore…at least not for now. It's kind of a shame. The timing is terrible."

"What do you mean when you say, 'not for now'?"

"After the incident with Richard and what happened the other night at the PMC Atlanta Children's Hospital, we know that we need to have some mechanism to track and monitor the elite. We just don't know what that looks like now. Everyone agreed that we needed to do something, but no one agreed on a course of action. For that matter, no one agreed where such a department should reside – FBI, CIA, Homeland Security, Department of Defense; there wasn't a clear place. Ultimately, the FBI took ownership, and it's now Bradshaw's responsibility to call the shots."

"So, what does that mean for you now?"

"Well, I have been asked to look into this hospital incident and then do file and location updates for all the elite as well as risk assessments for each one."

"Any leads on the hospital event yet?"

"I wish I could tell you about it, Tom, but…"

"Right. Sorry, George. I don't really work here anymore. Just old habits holding on I suppose."

"Your direct employment with the government, your benefits, access to classified information and clearance has been revoked. That said, as one of the few remaining experts on the elite, I left a window for you to return in the future as a contractor under certain circumstances. The conditions are difficult. It may never happen, so don't sit at home waiting for a phone call. It is also my responsibility to remind you that you are legally bound to the confidentiality documentation you agreed to and signed in the past, as well as the papers I will have you sign before you leave. You will receive a small severance package that should help you survive for a month or two until you find new employment. You will need to move on with life, Tom. I believe it will be a good change for you."

"Thank you, George."

"If you have any personal items in your office, please gather them; you'll need to be out by lunchtime."

"I will," Tom said as he stood and walked toward the door.

"Oh, and Tom."

"Yes, George."

"On a personal note, I was so happy to hear about the encounter in your back yard. I can see a change in you from the man you were before, and I am confident that there are great things in store for you in your future."

"Thanks again, George," Tom said as he left the conference room and made his way to the old office. Packing up his personal items didn't take long. Once everything was boxed up, Tom spent a few minutes sitting silently in his chair with his elbows on the desk and his hands folded up to his chin. He remembered how he felt the first time he lost his job. Now those feelings seemed so foreign. He was at peace with the consequences this time, knowing that it could have been much worse.

Chapter 6

Traffic was getting heavy, and Danielle was already running late. She was still ten miles from the highway exit that would lead her to the home that she shared with George for the past thirty years. She couldn't get home fast enough. They began their married life in a small starter home in East Point, but they later moved into the North Druid Hills neighborhood when their children were still small so they could be closer to the better school districts. The neighborhood was one of the few in the Atlanta area that seemed to retain its value. Their home wasn't large, but it had been big enough for them to raise their three children.

It was Friday night, and George had planned a special date for his bride of thirty-seven years. The commute home seemed to take much longer than usual, and Danielle exhaled with relief as she turned onto their neighborhood street. As she approached the house and turned into the driveway, she reached up to press the remote button for the garage door. Through the years, she had timed the motions perfectly so that the garage door was open just as her car reached the top of the driveway, but something wasn't quite right this time. She pushed the button several times, but the door seemed to ignore her. It had worked fine the day before, and she was sure the batteries were fresh.

She felt the tension in her shoulders as the car slowly approached the closed garage door. She stopped the car, closed her eyes, and took a deep breath trying to make herself calm down and resist the urge to be stressed. She turned the car keys, pulled them from the ignition, and held them tight as she opened the car door to make her way toward the front door of the house.

As she approached the front door, she noticed that it was cracked open slightly. At first, she thought this may have all been part of some romantic surprise that George had planned. He was persistent in his attempts to keep the passion alive in their marriage, and although it didn't always work out the way he had planned it, she cherished his relentless pursuit of her affections.

Her anticipation as she approached the door disappeared immediately, and her heart sank within her as she slowly pushed the front door open.

"Hello," she said softly as the door swung on its hinges. There was no reply.

The messy condition of the living room left her speechless. She carefully stepped onto the small section of tile near the door that transitioned into carpet in their open living room. Both table lamps were shattered on the ground and everything in their entertainment center had been spilled out on the floor. There were no lights on anywhere in the house.

Her eyes scanned toward the left where the kitchen was located. She could see through the doorway that the kitchen was in shambles. Her breath became heavy as she called out in a quiet, crackly voice.

"George…George, are you there?"

Again, there was no reply. The fading sunlight through the windows was the only light in the house. Fear welled up inside her, and she froze for a few moments not knowing what to do. A lump had developed in her throat making it hard to breathe. She held her breath, and the eerie silence amplified the sound of her beating heart.

She stood silently with the front door still open behind her. Her mind was racing. Should she call the police? Should she continue in or run away? Where was George? What had happened here? The questions were coming too fast for her to think through a logical course of action. Suddenly, the silence was broken by a faint groan.

Instinctively, Danielle moved quickly from the living room to the hall on the right and toward the back of the house where the master bedroom was located. The groan was faint, but she knew it had come from the bedroom. As she briskly moved down the hall, she passed the other bedrooms where their children had played and lived. She glanced in each room only for a moment to see more disruption and destruction. Every room was completely ransacked.

The master bedroom was in the worst condition. There was abounding evidence of a struggle. All the dresser drawers had been left open, and clothes were strewn all over the place. Danielle's small work desk that sat in the corner of the bedroom had been demolished, leaving papers and old mail items scattered on the floor with clothes and broken picture frames. Her heart pounded as the sound of movement drew her attention to the floor near the footboard. She saw a slender, bare foot lying in an awkward position on the floor.

Danielle quickly clambered over their queen size bed to find George laying half-dressed and covered in blood from the neck down on the floor.

"George," she screamed as she hopped down to the floor next to his lifeless body. She was gripped with horror and tears flooded her eyes. She cradled his head in her arms as she kept repeating his name. Her body was shaking. She brushed his pale face as her tears dropped on his forehead.

"Oh God," she said, barely able to speak. "Oh God, no. Please. George. Please. No."

George's mouth opened slightly, revealing the small, short breath that was left in him. As a faint sound started coming from his mouth, Danielle leaned in close to listen.

"I love you, Danny." The voice was weak and barely understandable. George was struggling hard to make the sounds come out as life continued to fade from his body. "I have always loved you."

With those last words, George could fight no more. His head slumped back being supported only by Danielle's arms. She buried his lifeless head in her bosom and sobbed, begging God not to take his life. It was too late.

Chapter 7

George's funeral was simple but elegant. The pastor presided over a graveside service that could not have happened on a more beautiful day. Attendance at the funeral was evidence of how much impact George had on the lives of those around him. There were so many people that most attendees had to stand. They were lined up the hillside all dressed in black to pay their respects. Some were family and some were colleagues or church friends.

Danielle, her kids, and their families sat in front of the crowd solemn and quiet. There was a sense of sorrow mixed with pride around them. Tom arrived early enough to get a seat, but he quickly gave it up to an older couple who he assumed were relatives of George. The Monroe family arrived a few minutes before the service began and stood next to Tom. Words were few out of respect during the funeral service.

During the service, Tom learned a lot about George. It made him wish he hadn't brushed off George's repeated attempts through the years to talk about the deeper things of life.

After the service, there was a long line of people waiting to talk to Danielle and the family. After a quick goodbye and a warm hug from Suzanna, the Monroes quietly departed the scene, leaving Tom to internally debate his next move. Ultimately, he decided to wait in line to see Danielle, although he had no idea what to say to her.

After waiting in the slow-moving processional, Tom finally arrived near the grave site. He shook hands and offered his condolences to George's children and their families before approaching Danielle. Although she had spoken to so many people before Tom, she behaved like she was fresh with energy. Her eyes locked on his as he approached, and a sincere smile broke through the lines of tears on her face. She hugged him gently and kept hold of his hand while they spoke.

"Tom, thank you so much for coming. You were a special person in George's life."

"Thank you for the kind words, Danielle. I am so sorry about what happened. George meant a lot to me. I wish I had more time to thank him for everything he did for me. If you need anything at all, or if there is anything I can do for you or your family, please don't hesitate to ask."

Her eyes never left his, and her smile never faded. She nodded ever so gently as he spoke as if she was cherishing every word. She was still holding Tom's hand and reached in for a hug. As she pulled him tight, she brought her lips as close to his ear as possible and whispered, "Meet me at the Corner Café this Thursday at two o'clock."

Tom was caught off guard by her comment. It seemed so awkward in this moment of grieving. As she pulled back, her facial expression was the same as it had been during their brief conversation.

"Thank you again for your kindness, Tom. I do hope to see you again."

Tom was still a bit perplexed but thought that if she was going to play it off, then he should do the same. After one final consoling smile, he turned and left her to attend to her other guests.

Her words haunted him for the next few days. Perhaps she knew something about George's murder that she couldn't trust anyone with. That thought led Tom to research as much about the incident as he could. The local police treated it like a home robbery with a possible link to a gang initiation, but he wasn't sold on that story. As much as he thought about it and as many conspiracy scenarios as he explored, it all led to nothing short of speculation. Tom's curiosity would prove to be without resolution until his mysterious meeting with Danielle.

Chapter 8

Tom arrived at the Corner Café early unable to bear the burden of the mystery any longer. He ordered a bottled water and sat outside on the little patio next to the café. He watched as Danielle's car pulled into the parking lot. She emerged with her oversized purse and coffee cup in her hand. Her fashion sense was much more modern than George's had been and, although she was advanced in years, she pulled off a regal look that few women could.

She didn't waste any time going inside the café. She spotted Tom as she was driving in and walked around the side of the building where he was. She took a seat with Tom at the table after a quick glance to ensure that they were alone. She crossed her legs as Tom welcomed her.

"Danielle, are you okay?"

"Yes, Tom. I will be fine. Losing George was unexpected. I'm not going to tell you that it has been or ever will be easy, but I know the time we spent together was a gift. I will always be grateful for it. He was a good man to me and the kids."

"Still, I can't imagine what you are going through. You are very wise and resilient."

Danielle grimaced at that comment and sat back a little in her chair.

"I don't know that George would one hundred percent agree with you on that one Tom, but I appreciate the comment."

"What you said to me at the funeral has kept me in suspense these past few days."

She smiled.

"Yes, I'm sure it did. I'm sorry to spring that on you, but I've been a bit paranoid about the privacy of phone calls and meetings lately. I had to talk to you."

"Is this about how George was killed?"

"He always said you were a smart one, Tom. I don't believe the police reports about this being a botched robbery or a gang initiation."

"Honestly, Danielle, I don't either."

"Whoever those people were, they were looking for something."

"Do you know what they were looking for?"

She reached into her purse and pulled out an object. It was a thin black box that was about the same size as her hand. It had a small black cord attached to it.

"I believe this is what they were looking for," she said.

"What is it?"

"It's an external hard drive. Every so often, George would open up his work laptop, plug this in, and spend a few hours buried in his own little world."

"Do you know what is on it?"

"Not exactly. I know that it is related to the work he was doing, but it was a personal interest for him too."

"What do you mean?"

"In confidence, he told me a little about the elite. He was fascinated by the existence of supernatural ability. I think he was trying to figure out how this fit in to what he believed was the end times."

"End times?"

"He believed that the growing population of the elite might be a sign that history is coming to conclusion. He had several discussions with our pastor about it."

"Did he ever tell you what this little personal project was about?"

"Sometimes I wish he had; other times I wish I didn't know as much as I did. George was a man who had secrets in his career life. Whenever he got through working, he would unplug the hard drive and hide it in a small hole in the wall behind the headboard of our bed. There were a few times that curiosity got to me and I would ask him about it, but he never would tell me. He only said that the secrets he had to keep from me were to keep me safe. I believed him then, and I still do."

"Did you try plugging it into your computer?"

"I said I believed him, but I didn't say my curiosity didn't get the better of me. Of course I tried it. It asked me for a password and after I failed to guess it three times, it locked me out. Tom, I don't know what is on this hard drive, but I believe it is important. I believe my husband died protecting it."

Tom nodded as she handed him the hard drive.

"Danielle, I can have this analyzed and let you know…"

"No, Tom," she said as she interrupted him. The smile was still on her face, but there was a hint of anguish in her eyes. "The job that you do and the responsibilities you have – they were all part of our lives for much too long. George is gone, and I have made peace with that. I need to move on and spend the time I have left here with my family. I gave you this because I thought George would want you to have it, and I trust you with it."

Tom was humbled and perplexed. "I don't know what to say, Danielle."

"You don't need to say anything. George told me about the events that have been going on in your life, and he was convinced that you are committed to doing the right thing." Her expression suddenly became somber as she continued, "Tom, there was a point in our marriage when everything seemed to be falling apart.

George consumed himself with work and neglected his family. I was so upset at him that I almost left. George begged me for a second chance, and he committed to me that he was going to change. I was reluctant at first, but now I am so glad that I decided to give it a try. Our marriage and our life got so much better after that turning point. I wouldn't trade it for anything."

Tom sat back in his seat holding the device in his lap, but completely focused on her words.

"Tom, I firmly believe that everyone deserves a second chance. This is yours. I need you to honor my husband's sacrifice by taking this and promising me that you will handle this information the same way George would have handled it."

The burden of her request felt heavy on his shoulders. Although he had failed to be a man of integrity in his past, Tom had no other choice now than to use this as an opportunity to prove himself a changed man. He looked into her eyes with deep resolve.

"I will, Danielle, you have my word. Will you be okay?"

Her smile was warm, but sadness was in her eyes. "I will," she said as she rose from her chair. "Take care of yourself, Tom."

Tom stood as she turned and walked away. The meeting represented a turning point for her. A burden had been lifted, and she was free to begin the next phase of her life, a phase she would endure without her husband. What marked an ending for her marked a new beginning for Tom; a mystery to solve and answers to pursue.

Chapter 9

Tom Marshall Personal Log File BGEN4013

I couldn't get home fast enough after my meeting with Danielle. I pushed the accelerator a bit harder than normal, anxious to start digging into the mysterious side of George's life.

Surprisingly, I made it back to my house without a speeding ticket and walked quickly through my new, still unpainted, front door and into the little room off to the side where I had set up a home office. It wasn't anything fancy as I was usually at the office or out in the field during my time as a monitor. Now that my status and my job were gone, my pathetic little office represented the only familiar scene from my old life.

I eagerly plugged in the external hard drive. My excitement rose as my laptop instantly recognized the device and the icon popped up on my screen. I clicked on the icon revealing the single folder on the drive. It was labeled 'DON'.

"Who is Don?" I muttered to myself. To the best of my knowledge, George didn't know anyone named Don. I clicked on the folder and a window popped up asking for a password. I leaned back in my chair to think for a moment. As much as I knew about George, I had no clue where to even begin to guess at a password. I should have asked Danielle what she tried, but at the time I was too shocked by what she had told me. I resorted to talking myself through some obvious possibilities.

"This one is probably too easy," I said as I typed 'Danielle' and pressed the 'enter' key. Another window popped up on the screen with a disappointing message: 'Incorrect Password'.

I then started with the names of his children from oldest to youngest but was met with the same message. After three failed attempts, the field to enter a password was replaced with a timer that started at twenty-four hours. It began to count down in one-second intervals. Apparently, George or whoever set up the security on this file meant for a maximum of three login attempts every twenty-four hours.

I was not deterred so easily. I still had an entire suite of the government's most powerful cybersecurity tools on my laptop. With a smirk of arrogance, I clicked on the icon labeled 'Hound-dog'. This program had never failed to identify and crack password hashes in my previous work as a monitor. I was certain it would made quick work of George's hard drive. My confidence quickly waned when Hound-dog failed to even bypass the hard drive's login attempt settings.

My train of thought was interrupted by the familiar ring of my cell phone.

"Hello."

"Is this Tom Marshall?"

"Yes, it is."

"Good afternoon Tom, this is Greg Bradshaw with the FBI."

"Hello Mr. Bradshaw. George mentioned you in our last conversation."

"Please, call me Greg. I am sure you know that Mr. Miller has passed away."

"Yes, I attended his funeral on Tuesday."

"His death was very sudden and unexpected. Unfortunately, we still need to move forward, and George left a pretty large skill gap in an area that has recently gotten a lot of attention. When we talked last week, George made a strong recommendation that you be hired as a government contractor if certain conditions arose. George's departure was one of those conditions. I know this is short notice, but my leadership is expecting progress updates and risk assessments on the elite and there aren't many people with the right skill set to do the job effectively."

"I understand sir. I would be happy to help."

"Great. Can you meet with me briefly tomorrow morning at your old office complex?"

"Yes sir. I will be there at eight in the morning. Thank you sir."

"See you then, Tom."

I had mixed emotions about the conversation. The job was my dream come true, but it didn't happen the way I wanted it to. I wanted to work with George, not replace him. I couldn't change the circumstances though, and this opportunity could prove to be a catalyst to help me find out exactly what happened to George. Perhaps he had stumbled on something that ultimately led to his demise. Whatever it was, I was committed to find it and keep my word to Danielle.

Tom Marshall Personal Log File BGEN4013
End of Record

Chapter 10

Tom was very anxious to get started. He decided to always keep George's external hard drive with him, just in case someone came looking for it.

He entered the familiar building and walked to the conference room where Mr. Bradshaw was waiting for him. Greg Bradshaw looked to be in his fifties. He was clean shaven and had eyes that appeared larger than normal. His haircut was short, and it was easy to tell that baldness was setting in. The black suit, white shirt, and red tie he wore completed his well-groomed appearance. Tom entered the room and shook Greg's hand. His breath smelled like strong coffee when he spoke. After exchanging the typical "good morning" conversation, they both sat down, and Greg went straight into business mode.

Tom's meeting with Bradshaw was brief and straight to the point. He asked Tom to pick up where George had left off with the PMC Atlanta Children's Hospital investigation. He also requested that Tom provide updated summaries and risk assessments for the elite. He reinstated an interim security clearance profile, gave Tom a department credit card, and a travel budget.

"Any questions, Tom?"

"No sir, I understand what I need to do."

"Great. To be honest, Tom, despite what happened in the past, George was very insistent that you were trustworthy and self-sufficient. That is exactly what I need from you."

"I understand."

"This assignment was dropped onto my already busy workload, so I need your commitment that you'll handle things appropriately and this won't be an issue for me."

"Yes sir."

"You must keep the elite out of the public eye. We can't afford another potential incident like the one we faced with Richard. Maintain confidentiality, keep me updated, and stay out of trouble. If you can do that, everything will be just fine. Do you understand?"

"Yes sir."

"Very good. Send me progress updates every Friday afternoon so I can review them over the weekend and provide updates to my leadership each Monday morning. Meet your commitments, hit your deadlines, and I won't micromanage you."

"Yes sir, Mr. Bradshaw. You can count on me."

"I hope so, Tom."

Bradshaw stood, shook Tom's hand, and excused himself from the room.

Trying to pick up where George had left off took Tom most of the day. He worked diligently on the file updates as requested and kept a watchful eye on the clock. At times, it was difficult to stay focused. The building was so quiet and lonely. His mind kept wandering back to a time when there were agents walking up and down the corridor and the low rumble of activity permeated the air. Now, it was still and almost eerie.

At three o'clock, Tom grabbed his bag and pulled out the external hard drive to make another attempt at a password. The options had been running through his head since the day before. He still wasn't sure who 'DON' was but decided to try variations of Donna, Donald, and Donatello. Still no luck.

After spending a few more hours organizing the progress George had already made on the file updates, Tom decided to pack up for the day.

Chapter 11

Falling back into his workaholic routine, Tom spent Friday night and all day Saturday working on the investigation and file updates George had started. He remembered Danielle telling him to take advantage of his second chance. Unfortunately, the entire situation was yielding more questions than he could possibly answer on his own. By Saturday evening, he had made no progress on getting answers regarding George's death, the PMC Atlanta Children's Hospital event, or the mysterious 'DON' file on George's external hard drive. Failing at every turn and mentally exhausted, Tom fell asleep on his living room couch.

He woke to the sound of an alarm beeping from the office where he had left his phone. He sat up confused for a moment and then realized that it was Sunday.

Having learned his lesson from previous weeks, Tom arrived at the church early enough to get a good parking spot. He had also memorized which door Suzanna faithfully worked as a greeter each Sunday. Her pleasant demeanor made her perfect for the job, and it helped him feel like he was a part of something again.

Lunch with the Monroe family was much less awkward than the previous week. Jacob and Christina both seemed much more relaxed. They all gathered around the table and bowed their heads as Robert blessed the food.

"We were so sorry to hear about what happened to George," Robert said after ending his prayer.

"Me too," Tom replied. "As long as George and I worked together, I feel like there was so much more to him that I didn't know. There are so many questions I want to ask him."

"Has there been any progress on finding out who killed him?" Robert asked.

"Not that I know of."

With that statement, Tom's face became downcast as if he were struggling within himself to reconcile the events of George's death.

"It just doesn't make any sense," Tom said.

"What doesn't make sense?"

"George was a good man and a strong leader. He had a family who loved him and a purpose in his life. I spent my whole life chasing meaningless things and manipulating people and circumstances for my own gain. But here we are. I am alive and free, and George is gone. It doesn't seem fair. I don't deserve any of this. How do you do it?"

"How do we do what?" Robert replied.

"You're all great and you try to do the right thing, but through no fault of your own, tragedy still strikes your family. It doesn't seem fair. It seems like you deserve better, but you still accept what has happened without being resentful. I just don't understand."

"Well, Tom, I can't say that we don't struggle with it at times, but sometimes God uses things that don't seem fair to build our faith."

Tom looked up as Robert continued.

"The man with strong faith yields to the fact that God gets to do things the way He wants them, even if it doesn't seem fair."

"I don't know if I'll ever understand that," Tom said with a slight grin.

"Well, Mr. Marshall, you are in good company," Jacob said.

"Please, Jacob, call me Tom."

"Yes sir, Tom. I've been meaning to ask you something if you don't mind."

"Sure"

"How many other people are there like me?"

"I don't have an exact number, but I'm sure I'll have a better idea once I get through all of the file updates."

"File updates?"

"The department—well, I guess that's just me—now answers to the FBI. With the recent incidents, they want location and file updates on all the elite."

"That sounds tedious," Jacob said before taking another bite.

"It can be, but I really enjoy it. Not having a family of my own, I have always considered the elite to be my family in a weird sort of way."

"Well, Tom Marshall," Suzanna said with a smile, "you've got a family now whether you want one or not." Tom smiled.

"Thank you, Suzanna. And regarding your question, Jacob, I'm sure there can't possibly be too many just like you."

The harmless jab of banter lightened the mood and was well received. Jacob looked up and grinned, and Christina chuckled quietly. After finishing off the meal with warm apple cobbler, Tom thanked them, said goodbye, and walked out to the front porch. He paused a moment at the edge of the steps when he heard the front door open behind him.

"Mr. Marshall...I mean Tom."

He turned to see Jacob. He could tell by the look on his face there was something serious on his mind. Tom shifted over to lean on the porch railing and looked him straight in the eye.

"What is it, Jacob?"

"My dad always told me that it takes a real man to stand up, admit when he is wrong, and ask for forgiveness."

"Well, it didn't come easy; I was scared to death that you…"

"Oh, I didn't come out here to talk about your apology, Tom, I came to talk about mine."

"Yours?"

"Yes sir. When everything happened, and I realized that it wasn't just an accident, I let myself fill up with anger. It consumed me like I had never felt before. I felt such rage and I wanted personal justice so bad that I lost control. I was ready to hurt you…really bad."

"I think under the circumstances, Jacob, your anger was warranted."

"Maybe Tom, but letting it control me and coming after you like that; it wasn't right. I need to man up and apologize for my behavior. I shouldn't have treated you like that. I am sorry."

Tom was astonished. After all the pain he had caused Jacob and his family, Jacob was standing before him and apologizing for his behavior. Tom held his stare in Jacob's eyes and extended his hand.

"Jacob, I really don't' think you need to apologize here, but I admire you for your convictions. Please consider the whole incident forgiven and forgotten."

"Thank you, Tom," Jacob said as he shook his hand, "It's forgiven and forgotten on my end too."

65

A great burden fell from both their shoulders that day. Tom had lost an enemy and gained a friend in Jacob Monroe.

Chapter 12

George didn't leave many clues for Tom to find regarding the miracle at the PMC Atlanta Children's Hospital, but he had ordered a full autopsy on the mysterious figure found in the stairwell. Tom received an email stating that the autopsy was complete and ready for review. Bradshaw had arranged for all of George's email to be routed to Tom. Tom hated visiting the morgue, but it was necessary to confirm his suspicions that the young man was indeed a Class 2 elite with healing abilities.

The reinstatement of his government credentials by Bradshaw, although more limited than he had in the past, came in handy at the morgue. He quickly found the medical examiner and requested to see the body. Tom was escorted by the medical examiner back to an area he called the "cold room". It was a large room painted dull grey with a messy desk at one end and rows of tables on the other. Some of the tables were occupied while others were empty. The room felt like a freezer, and Tom crossed his arms to help keep himself warm. The medical examiner was an older gentleman who wore a shirt and tie beneath his lab coat and remained emotionless through the entire visit.

"Here's the final report on the body," the medical examiner said as he directed Tom to the table where the young man was laid covered with a sheet.

"Have you made a positive identification and contacted his relatives?"

"Well now, that is the interesting part. We do know who he is. Joshua Goodson. Lived with his mother; father wasn't in the picture at all."

"Sounds too familiar these days."

"Yes, but here's the weird part, his mom came in a couple days earlier."

"A couple days ago? Did she come in looking for him? Was he missing?"

"No, she was brought in a couple days before he was," he said clarifying his statement, "She came in a bag."

The medical examiner motioned for Tom to follow him to the other side of the room where another body was laid and covered with a sheet.

"This is his mom, Ashley Goodson; thirty-two years old, single lady with no medical issues."

"Mind if I take a look?" Tom asked.

"Not at all, just don't touch anything," he said as he walked back toward his desk at the other end of the room.

Tom thought it was odd that the medical examiner's desk was in the cold room. He lifted the corner of the sheet and instantly recognized the face. It was Jennifer's friend Ashley. Tom remembered meeting her after the failed attempt to capture Richard at Camp Pennington. He also remembered noticing Joshua's restrainer chip before they left Jennifer's apartment.

Tom walked briskly back over to the table where Joshua's body was and lifted the corner of the sheet to confirm his suspicions. It was, in fact, the same Joshua he had met a few weeks earlier. The medical examiner sat at his desk several feet away but still within earshot. He was filling out some forms on a clipboard. Tom pulled back the sheet exposing the boy's head and bent down to try to get a good look at the back of his head. The vantage point didn't give him a good view. He glanced up to see if the medical examiner was watching, but he was engrossed in his paperwork. Tom pulled a pen from his pocket and used it to try to rotate Joshua's head so he could get a better look at the chip implant location. The head was stiff, and Tom could feel the coldness coming from the skin. With some extra force, the head rotated just enough for Tom to examine the upper part of his neck. After another quick glance to ensure he wasn't being watched, he held his breath and leaned in closer to examine the body.

The difficulty Tom had turning Joshua's head coupled with the site of lifeless bodies and the smell of the room made him very queasy. He used his pen to move some of the hair around the implant location. It looked undisturbed.

The chip is still there, but it must have malfunctioned, Tom thought to himself as he stood back upright and covered the body once more with the sheet.

"Is there any link between these deaths?" Tom asked.

"Not for me to determine," the medical examiner said not looking up from his writing, "I let the investigators handle that."

"What's the story on her?" Tom asked.

"They found her tied up and gagged in an old abandoned warehouse. Poor girl looked like she had been tortured. She was missing a few fingers when she came in. There are some sick people in the world. Her white blood cell count at the time of death was higher than I have ever seen; completely off the charts."

"We have reason to believe there are some security risks with both of these victims. I am going to authorize both of these bodies to be transferred to a federal facility for processing."

"Ok," the medical examiner said with a slightly puzzled look on his face.

"How can I get a copy of the autopsy report for the woman?"

The medical examiner shuffled around on his desk for a minute before pulling one sheet from a disorganized pile of papers.

"Here, just fill this out and leave it with me."

"Thanks."

Tom completed the form and pinned it to the corkboard that hung on the wall next to the desk. He supposed that there would be less of a chance for the disorganized medical examiner to lose it than if he had just placed it on the desk. Tom discarded his pen in the trash can next to the desk and thanked the medical examiner for his hospitality before leaving to go get some much-needed fresh air.

Tom tried putting some of the pieces together as he walked to his car. *Clearly Joshua had somehow discovered his elite status. Somehow his chip had malfunctioned or broken,* Tom thought.

Joshua would often help his mom at the hospital after school and was friends with many of the children there. Tom assumed that maybe Joshua saw his healing ability as a way to help his friends. What Tom couldn't reconcile was how Joshua's death or Ashley's death tied into the bigger question – why?

Chapter 13

Tom had too many puzzle pieces in his head and none of them seemed to fit together. He tried three passwords every day to access George's hard drive, but the 'incorrect password' prompt persistently taunted him each day. He wasn't any closer to a viable theory about George's death or Joshua's restrainer chip. Nothing seemed to be adding up. The information he learned at the morgue prompted him to cross reference recent deaths involving former elite with deaths involving their family members. It wasn't long before his search led to Riley Nicole Bridges.

Riley was a Class 2 elite with healing abilities. She was seventeen years old and one of Tom's former clients. Her mom died due to complications when Riley was born, and she was raised by her father until she was six years old. At the time, she didn't understand why her dad sent her to live with her grandmother in Charlotte. When Riley was eight years old, she received word that her father had lost his two-year battle with an aggressive type of cancer. Although she experienced so much loss in her young life, Riley was kindhearted and joyful. Through his periodic checks on her, Tom watched her grow up and navigate the trials life handed her. She was an extremely attractive young lady with fair skin and piercing brown eyes. Her cautious personality made it easy for Tom to keep track of her and rate her as a low risk for incidents.

Tom pulled the old records on Riley. His research revealed that Riley's grandmother, Elaine Bridges, was found dead in her apartment at the beginning of the month. There was no reference of Riley in any of the reports, but Tom felt in his gut that something terrible had happened. He packed a small bag, reserved a hotel near Charlotte, and left as quickly as he could. Tom knew that he would arrive in Charlotte too late in the evening to start searching for Riley, but he wanted to begin as early as possible in the morning.

Tom started at Elaine's apartment, but there was no trace of Riley anywhere. He checked with her school, but no one had seen her or heard from her all month. The principal told Tom that some other people had come looking for Riley right after Christmas break, but nobody had been back since then. There were over three thousand students registered in the high school and the senior class had chronic absentee rate, so the staff dismissed her disappearance as another high school dropout.

The morning disappeared quickly as Tom kept running into dead ends. He was getting hungry but didn't want to stop searching. He visited the homeless shelter where Riley would often volunteer with her grandmother on the weekends. As soon as he walked in the door, he recognized a familiar face sitting in the far corner of the room.

As his eyes locked onto hers, she jumped up and took off running toward the back door.

"Riley, wait," Tom yelled as he chased after her.

Riley darted out of the back door of the shelter and ran down the alley. Tom did his best to keep up, but he was slowly losing ground to Riley, who was much younger and in better shape. She ran across the road dodging oncoming cars and down the next alley with Tom not too far behind. The alley was a dead end. In a panic, she quickly glanced around for an exit and started climbing a nearby ladder to the roof of an old building. Tom followed, still losing ground.

As he reached the top of the ladder, Riley was already on the opposite side of the roof. There were no stairs near her and the jump to the next building looked too far to risk. Riley trembled with fear as she inched closer to the edge of the roof looking down at the thirty-foot drop that seemed to be her only option for escape.

"Riley, stop," Tom yelled, "Your grandmother's name was Elaine." He walked slowly toward her still trying to catch his breath, "Your mother passed away at childbirth and your father died of cancer when you were only eight years old."

Riley stopped. She didn't turn around to look at Tom, but her body stood still as she listened carefully. Her hair shifted softly in the breeze. Tom continued toward her slowly as he spoke.

"There's a scar on the inside of your left leg just above your ankle. You got it when you were four years old. Your dad took you for a ride on his motorcycle and your leg touched the hot engine."

Riley stayed still as a tear fell from her eye. Tom continued talking as he slowly approached her.

"You wore glasses when you were little, but your eyes got better as you got older. You told everyone that you just outgrew them. You taught yourself how to crochet when you were twelve years old, but everyone assumed your grandmother taught you. You never corrected them because you knew it made Elaine happy when people gave her the credit. When you took the driving test to get your license, you had to sit on a pillow because you were shorter than other girls your age."

"Who are you?" Riley asked in a crackled voice.

"My name is Tom. I am your friend, Riley. There's a lot I need to explain to you, but what you need to understand right now is I only want to help you."

Riley stepped away from the roof edge, collapsed to the ground, and began crying. Tom carefully approached her, kneeled beside her, and put his arm around her shoulders.

"I don't have anyone left," Riley said trying to catch her breath as she sobbed, "I don't have anywhere to go."

"I know, Riley. Please, let me help you. I promise not to hurt you."

There was something soothing about Tom's voice. It was evident that she was traumatized by recent events in her life including the death of her grandmother. She knew she had already spent too long hiding in fear, and she needed someone to help her understand what was happening. Her instinct was to trust Tom, but she couldn't explain why she should put faith in a man she just met. She didn't really have any better options.

Riley was silent for a few moments. After regaining her composure, she slowly stood to her feet. Tom helped her up not knowing what to say next.

"What happens now?" she asked wiping the remaining moisture from her face.

"Now, we take the safer route back down to the ground. Then, I buy us both some lunch," Tom said trying to lighten the mood. Her small smile was enough evidence that it worked.

"That sounds like a good start," she replied, "what then?"

"I'd like to take you back with me."

"Where?"

"Somewhere safe."

"Okay," she replied.

"Do you have any clothes or anything you need to take with you?"

"All I have is what you see."

"Well, that's a problem. I think I know who can help with that though."

Chapter 14

Tom was anticipating an interesting ride back to Atlanta. He felt as though Riley could be a key part of solving some of the mysteries he was trying to figure out. There wasn't much conversation during lunch. Riley's hunger took precedence over her manners. She consumed her chicken sandwich faster than Tom had ever seen a seventeen-year-old girl eat. While she was finishing her fries, Tom excused himself to make a phone call.

"Hello, Tom."

"Hi, Robert. Do you have a minute to talk?"

"I do. Is everything okay?"

"Yes. I have a huge favor to ask of you though."

"Well, fire away. We'll do our best to help you out."

"I'm leaving Charlotte on my way back home right now. I have a teenage girl named Riley with me who needs a place to stay for a little while."

"Ok," Robert said, "what about this are you not telling me?"

"There's a lot I don't know yet. She is a Class 2, and her family is gone. I think something bad happened and she's been hiding out for a couple of weeks now. She needs a safe and secure place to stay until we can figure out what's going on. Can you and Suzanna help out?"

"Of course, Tom, please bring her over."

"We won't get there until later this evening."

"Not a problem, Suzanna will prepare the guest room and we'll stay up waiting for your arrival."

After ending his phone conversation, Tom stowed his phone and returned to Riley.

"Ready to go?" Tom asked.

"Yes sir," she replied as she stood and followed Tom to his car.

Once Tom maneuvered onto the interstate, he planned to strike up a conversation with Riley to get some information. He was disappointed to see that she had reclined the seat back all the way and was fast asleep. She looked too peaceful to disturb, so Tom turned down the volume on the radio and let her rest.

As they drove through downtown Atlanta, Riley flinched as if she were jumping out of a bad dream. The sudden movement startled Tom, making him swerve to stay in his lane.

"Are you okay?" Tom asked.

"Yeah, just a bad dream. Where are we?"

"Driving through Atlanta on our way to Griffin, Georgia. I have some friends there who are going to take you in for a few days."

Riley stayed very quiet. Her eyes glazed over.

"Are you okay?" Tom asked.

"I just don't want to be back here again."

"Back where?"

She didn't answer.

Realizing he had struck an emotional nerve, Tom opted to change the subject.

"When was the last time you got a good night's sleep?"

"It's been a while. I guess not since last month," Riley paused, "before they took me."

"Who took you? What happened?"

Riley sat silently. Tom's questions made her remember the trauma she had been through over the past few weeks. Her body language became defensive as if she had quickly constructed an emotional wall between her and Tom.

"I'm sorry, Riley. I told you I was your friend, so I need to act like a better one. If you don't want to talk about it right now, that's okay. I don't want to put you on the spot. Is there anything you want to ask me?"

"Let's start with…who are you and how do you know so much about me?"

"My name is Tom Marshall. I used to work for the government as a monitor for special people like you."

"Monitor? Like babysitting?"

"No, more like watching and observing. And taking lots of notes."

"That sounds like babysitting."

"Hmmm. I guess it does," Tom chuckled.

"So, everyone is being watched by the government?"

"No. Just the special people."

Riley's face was perplexed. "I'm not special," she said,

"You *are* special, Riley. You just don't know it yet."

"What is special about me?"

Tom paused. He knew he had to win Riley's trust, but he also needed to maintain the confidentiality of the elite. Realizing that he had spent too much of his life prioritizing his job over relationships, Tom continued.

"Can I trust you with a secret?"

Riley finally turned her head toward him and nodded.

"It all started forty years ago with a baby boy named John Pennington. John had a genetic deviation that made him very strong and very tough. Sadly, that same gift ended up taking his life. He wasn't the only one. There were others born with similar deviations who had different gifts, but like John, they died. After John, doctors and scientists developed a tiny microchip called a restrainer chip for other special children born with similar gifts."

"Wait a minute. Are you saying I am like him? Do I have a restrainer chip? Am I going to die? Did my mom and dad know about this? Did my grandmother know? Is that why they came for me?"

"That's a lot of questions all at once," Tom said intentionally interrupting. "You have a genetic deviation like John, but yours is different. You do have a restrainer chip, but you're not going to die because of it. Once the restrainer chip is in place, everyone who has it grows up just like any other person and doesn't even realize they have a genetic anomaly. Your family didn't know anything about it. None of the families were ever told. Well, almost none. You're going to stay with an older couple named Robert and Suzanna Monroe for a couple of days until we get this all sorted out. They know about the special gifts and the restrainer chips. In fact, their daughter was one of the first with a special gift. They also have a son who is special like you. He was one of the first to get a restrainer chip. He grew up perfectly normal and is now twenty-nine years old. They are going to take real good care of you. I can answer more of your questions after you recover for a few days."

Riley seemed content to end the conversation. Tom could tell that she was still trying to process all the information he just gave her.

The remainder of the ride to Griffin was peaceful and quiet. Just as Robert promised, the front porch light was on, and both he and Suzanna were waiting at the front door when Tom arrived.

After a long day, Riley showered and dressed in a spare pair of pajamas that Christina had left at Robert's house. She then buried herself in the blankets of the guest room bed and fell asleep quickly. Tom thanked Robert again for their generous hospitality and drove home to get some much-needed rest. There were a lot of unanswered questions, and a lot of research to do when he got home.

Chapter 15

Riley awoke to the smell of scrambled eggs as the sun shone past the window blinds and onto the foot of the bed. Eating dinner on the road the night before left a terrible taste in her mouth and falling asleep with wet hair made her look like a wild jungle girl. She heard a faint knock on the door as it slowly opened.

"Good morning, Riley."

"Good morning, Mrs. Monroe"

Riley was a bit embarrassed by her appearance and morning breath, but Suzanna kept her focus on Riley's eyes as she continued her morning greeting.

"I've got fresh eggs and waffles for breakfast, is that okay?"

"Yes ma'am. That sounds perfect."

"Great. I washed your clothes from last night and set them on the chair in the corner. Whenever you're ready, you can get dressed and come have some breakfast."

"Thank you so much."

"And after breakfast, you, me, and my daughter-in-law are going shopping. How does that sound?"

"So good, Mrs. Monroe. So good."

It wasn't long before Suzanna, Riley, and Christina were wandering through the clothing stores at the mall. Riley and Christina quickly became friends and the whole experience gave Riley a break from being thrust into adulthood.

When they arrived back at Christina's house, Suzanna retrieved Christina's wheelchair while Riley and Christina schemed together in the car.

"Mom, why don't you let Riley stay with us for a few days?" Christina asked as she maneuvered into the wheelchair.

"I don't know, sweetheart. She's already had so much change in her life recently."

"She would be a big help around the house," Christina said as she gave Suzanna the puppy-dog eyes, "you know I can't reach the top cabinets in the kitchen anymore."

"I guess it would be better for her to be around somebody closer to her age."

Christina quickly turned her head toward the car and said, "Hey, Riley, how would you like to stay for a few days?"

Riley's face lit up as she nodded in agreement.

"Why do I feel like you both planned this behind my back?" Suzanna asked. "Grab your bags, Riley, and when you get tired of the party scene at Christina's house, you just give me a call. Okay?"

"Yes ma'am," she replied as she jumped out of the car and loaded up Christina's lap with her new wardrobe. "Thank you again for…"

"Please dear, don't mention it. Now you go have some fun and don't worry about a thing."

Riley smiled as she turned to grab the handles of Christina's wheelchair and pushed her up the homemade ramp to the front door.

"That was so much fun Mrs.…."

"Oh no," Christina said interrupting, "please call me Christina. I appreciate your manners, but I'm not that much older than you, so there's no need to make me feel like an old lady."

"Yes ma'am. I mean, yes, Christina."

"Today was a lot of fun, wasn't it?"

"It was. Thank you so much. It helped me get my mind off…"

Riley's demeanor changed as she recalled the events of the last few weeks.

"Hey," Christina said, grabbing Riley's hand, "don't go dark on me now. Let's get those tags off your new clothes so we can give Jacob a fashion show when he gets home from work."

"Okay," Riley said, suppressing the negative emotions that consumed her life recently.

"Can I ask you about Jacob?"

"Sure you can. What would you like to know?"

"Mr. Marshall said that he was special, like me."

"Well, that's not really a question, but I think I know what you are looking for. Like you, Jacob was born with special abilities. He is extraordinarily strong. He didn't know it for a long time because he had a restrainer chip like yours. Then we got in a car accident that broke his restrainer chip and my back." Christina paused. She remembered the car accident that took more than her ability to walk and her countenance faded. Losing their child was still too painful for Christina to mention so she stopped short of finishing the story.

Riley was listening but focused on matching up her new outfits. "So, then what happened?" An awkward pause filled the room.

"Christina?"

"Oh, sorry," she said snapping back to reality, "well, he was able to use his strength to rescue me from a really bad situation. Then he swept me off my feet, and we are going to live happily ever after."

"Sounds dreamy," Riley said sarcastically.

"You'll get to see for yourself. He'll be home soon."

Chapter 16

Tom's newly established Sunday routine of church and lunch with the Monroe family seemed to represent the only stability in his life. It was the only time that he felt comfortable and secure. He walked into the small church and smiled as he saw Riley sitting with Jacob and Christina. The sermon seemed to hit Tom straight in the face. The pastor was preaching a series on the second coming of Christ. Tom was fascinated by the topic and was taking as many notes as possible. The pastor read from chapter twenty-four in Matthew.

"No one knows about that day or hour, not even the angels in heaven, nor the Son, but only the Father…"

Well, that makes me feel better. I'm not the only one with unanswered questions, Tom thought to himself as the pastor continued.

"As it was in the days of Noah, so will it be at the coming of the Son of Man…"

The days of Noah. That was one of George's sayings, Tom thought. He tuned out the pastor for a minute or two as the phrase brought memories of George to his mind. He recalled several circumstances in the past years when George would attempt to engage him in spiritual matters and use the phrase 'days of Noah' to describe the current culture. Before Tom knew it, the pastor had finished reading the Scripture selection and had moved on to the rest of his sermon. Tom wrote down the Scripture reference along with the words 'days of Noah' on the note sheet he was using.

He glanced up to make eye contact with the pastor and, as if his brain was moving a few minutes slower than his eyes, he looked back down at those words – 'days of Noah'. Tom glanced over at Suzanna's open Bible and the words seemed to jump out at him. His eyes widened as the realization hit him. 'DON' wasn't a person or a place, it was an abbreviation of a phrase. Tom was astounded. It was right there the whole time.

Lunch was delicious and appropriately timed for Tom. He had a lot of questions and, with George gone, Robert and Jacob were the only men he felt like he could trust with Biblical questions. After Suzanna put the last place on the table and Robert prayed over the meal, Tom immediately began the interrogation.

"So, what exactly does the 'days of Noah' mean?" he asked Robert, not trying to seem too eager.

"Well, Tom, it is a reference back to Genesis chapter six before the flood."

Tom hadn't really had much church exposure, but he did know about the flood. Without realizing it, his facial expression was screaming for more of an explanation. Robert continued.

"It was a bad time in the history of mankind. Everybody was doing whatever they wanted to do without any regard for God. The Bible says that every inclination of man was evil, and that God was grieved because of mankind's wickedness."

"So how does that relate to now?"

"The Bible says that in the last days, the world will be that bad again. People will do whatever they want without regard for God and wickedness will abound."

"George used the phrase 'days of Noah' quite a bit."

"I can see why," Robert replied as he spoke between bites. "I've seen the world get progressively worse as I get older. In Noah's day, he was the only one among all the people who was blameless and walked with God. I think we have more than just one righteous person on earth right now, but I still see how wickedness has dominated our society."

"I guess I would have to agree," Tom said. Not only did Tom agree, but he also recognized that for most of his life, he was a part of the growing wickedness.

"That is why we have to remain diligent and watchful for Christ's return," Robert said finishing his last bite of mashed potatoes.

"Would you happen to have a Bible that I could borrow for a little bit?" Tom asked. He was somewhat ashamed that he had gone to church with them for several weeks without having purchased one of his own.

"Of course, Tom," Robert said with a smile.

After a healthy slice of Suzanna's pecan pie, Tom excused himself to go home and do some reading. Robert handed him a Bible on his way out the door.

"Please call me if you have any questions," Robert said as he left.

"I will, Robert. And thank you."

Chapter 17

Tom wasn't sure if he could have categorized this event as a divine revelation, but he did know that the mystery of the password on George's hard drive had been frustrating him for a long time. He could not figure it out on his own. The timing of the pastor's sermon was no accident.

He arrived home with more than thirty minutes to spare before he could make another hard drive password attempt. He chose to use that time to catch up on some background behind the days of Noah and the flood. Tom kicked off his shoes and made himself comfortable on the living room couch. Since the account of the flood began in chapter six, he decided to start with the first chapter of Genesis to read in context. The reading captivated him and before he knew it an hour had passed.

Genesis 6:4 captured his attention. "The Nephilim were on the earth in those days, and also afterward, when the sons of God went to the daughters of humans and had children by them. They were the heroes of old, men of renown." Tom was a bit lost. He never considered himself a Bible scholar, but he did have a talent for figuring things out. Nevertheless, this verse had him completely baffled. He decided to take Robert up on the offer to help.

"Hello."

"Robert, hi, it's Tom."

"Good afternoon, Tom."

"Good afternoon. Sorry to bother you on a Sunday, but I was reading the Bible you gave me and had a question."

"Sure, Tom."

"I was reading Genesis chapter six and came across a verse and a word that I don't understand. It says the Nephilim were on the earth in those days and that the sons of God had children with the daughters of men. Do you know what any of that means?"

"You didn't start with an easy question, Tom. This is one of those mysteries of the Bible that we don't really have a good answer for. Some people believe that the 'sons of God' were angels who had children with humans and others believe that the 'sons of God' were descendants of Seth and strong followers of God who intermarried with descendants of Cain. All we really know for sure is what the Bible says about them."

"What does it mean when it says, 'heroes of old' and 'men of renown'?"

"I wish I had some better answers for you, Tom. Some believe that these people were giants or superhuman, but the reality is that we can't know for certain on this side of heaven. It is safe to say that if God leaves it as a mystery in the Bible, then we don't really need to know right now."

"I guess you're right."

"As you read and learn more, be careful that you don't get caught up in some of the mysteries of the Bible. They are fascinating to be sure, but we are called to dedicate our lives to loving God and loving others. We aren't called to chase after the unknown."

"I understand, Robert, thanks for your help."

"Of course, Tom. Please feel free to call anytime. I hope to see you next Sunday."

"I'll be there, Robert. Thanks again."

Tom was moderately disappointed that Robert didn't have a clear answer to his question. As much as he tried to ignore the verse and read on, his mind kept coming back to it. The word 'Nephilim' and the meaning behind it intrigued him. He couldn't help but think it may have intrigued George as well.

Tom set the Bible down on the end table, picked his shoes up off the floor, and walked to the bedroom to put them away. The whole time he kept thinking about the words he had read and wondered if George had felt the same draw to this part of Scripture. Perhaps he had made a correlation in his head between the 'days of Noah', the presence of a special group of people, and the current existence of the elite.

This was the best lead he had so, crossing his fingers, Tom walked to his little home office to make another attempt at the password. He logged in to his laptop, plugged in the hard drive, and clicked the icon to bring up the password entry field. He slowly typed the words 'days of Noah'. The familiar error message appeared on the screen as Tom's eyebrows furrowed. He sat for a moment staring at the screen. He knew he only had two more chances with the password before he was locked out for another day. Suddenly, a thought entered his head. He went back to the living room to pick up the Bible. He wanted to make sure his spelling was correct. Carefully, he typed the word 'Nephilim'. He paused to double-check the spelling before he pushed the enter key and hoped for the best.

The password request window disappeared. Tom sat still for a moment and stared at the screen not knowing what to expect. The folder remained on his screen. After a few moments, nothing happened. He was almost in disbelief as he clicked on the 'DON' folder. It immediately opened, revealing three subfolders. They were labeled in the following order:

K Wagner

Monitors

Elite Backup Files

Anxious to see what secrets George had hidden, he clicked on the subfolder, 'K Wagner'. It was a large folder on the hard drive and had many subfolders under the main folder. The more he read, the more he was shocked. George had originated some of the documents in the file decades ago. Tom pieced together a story that may have been George's biggest secret. It all started more than thirty-five years ago with a girl named Kylie Wagner.

Chapter 18

Kylie Wagner was an attractive, young black girl who grew up in a predominantly white neighborhood. Her father was a lawyer and her mother, who had a doctorate degree in mathematics, was a college professor. Kylie's upbeat personality and wealthy background led her to be naïve to the desires and deceitfulness of young men her age. At a time when the need for a monitoring department was just being realized, Kylie became pregnant. She was only sixteen years old, and the unexpected event in her life turned her whole world upside down.

Her parents navigated through the typical emotional roller coaster that accompanies an unexpected teen pregnancy. Initial anger evolved into rejection and fear. As the weeks and months passed, they made strides toward rebuilding the strained relationship. They encouraged Kylie to do the right thing, but their initial reaction in the first few weeks after the pregnancy test had already caused significant emotional damage.

Together, Kylie and her family went through weeks of anticipation, ridicule, and fear. She contemplated abortion on several occasions knowing that a decision to keep the baby boy developing inside her would change her life and her future forever.

After recovering from their initial failure to support her, Kylie's parents remained steadfast in their encouragement for her to have the baby. They offered to help raise him, but she continued to struggle with her own fears about the future.

At just over seven months pregnant, Kylie yielded to the worries that overwhelm a young teenage expectant mother. Confused and terrified, she made her way to the back-alley office of Dr. Travius Roe who specialized in preying off young girls and ignoring the laws of parental consent. After signing several forms that she didn't bother to read or understand, Kylie was escorted to a small back room. The whole place had a stale smell and didn't appear to be sanitary for any medical procedure, but Kylie's fear had gripped her beyond the point of rational thought.

She was quickly and quietly prepped for the medical procedure by Dr. Roe's assistant nurse Wanda who stayed in the room but remained silent while they waited for the doctor to enter. Kylie began sweating and her face turned clammy. Her pupils were dilated, and her breathing was heavy as she gazed at the stained ceiling tile in the room.

After a few minutes, Dr. Roe walked briskly into the room and, without acknowledging Kylie at all, immediately positioned himself for the procedure. As the doctor was putting on his gloves, Wanda wheeled over the metal cart that was lined on the top with his instruments. Kylie's legs twitched, and her eyes rolled back toward the top of her head. Almost instantly the twitching became shaking as her whole body jerked on the table. Wanda repositioned herself at Kylie's side trying to hold her steady and stared at Dr. Roe with anxiety in her eyes.

Dr. Roe quickly ran out of the room and entered again just a few seconds later with a syringe as Kylie's seizure continued. He launched the needle into her arm and commanded Wanda to hold her legs as still as she could. Wanda moved toward the end of the table and was shocked to see the tiny head of Kylie's baby boy. Her stunned look caught the doctor's attention and he quickly moved in place to help facilitate the rest of the delivery.

Once the baby was born, Kylie's seizure stopped, and she lay motionless on the table. Neither the infant nor his mother moved. Dr. Roe passed the baby onto Wanda and told her to take care of it while he attended to Kylie. Even if he had been a reputable doctor, there was nothing he could have done to save her. The breath of life had left Kylie Wagner. Dr. Roe stood next to her lifeless body not knowing what to do. Wanda slowly backed out of the room with the limp, under-developed little body wrapped in a white towel.

She took the baby into another room and laid him on the table, still in shock from what she just witnessed. Her heart was beating fast and hard as she gazed wide-eyed at the table. Suddenly, a small movement captured her attention. She stepped toward the table and leaned over to see the little chest moving up and down. Without a cry or any other signs of life, somehow this tiny baby was breathing.

Wanda had spent her career convincing herself that unborn children were simply a collection of tissue with no life or emotion, but as she watched the baby boy lying helpless on the table, her whole view changed. His eyes were not open, and he still made no sound but there seemed to be sadness in his face. Wanda was overcome with emotion and began crying. She grabbed a fresh towel, wrapped the baby snugly and walked briskly out the front door with tears streaming down her eyes. She got into her car with the newborn on her lap and started driving. She didn't know where she was going or what she should do, but she knew that she had to leave that place. She decided that day she would never return.

Kylie's parents were crushed when they received the phone call from Dr. Roe's office. They were told that both Kylie and the baby had died. The autopsy report on Kylie showed that she died from a psychogenic nonepileptic seizure. Kylie's father used his legal prowess to strip the doctor of his license and his livelihood. In the process of losing his career, Dr. Roe purged all files and documentation from his clinic. The clinic was closed and never reopened.

Wanda drove for almost an hour after the incident. Every few minutes, she would reach down with her hand to feel the baby still breathing. She had never witnessed anything so unusual and life changing. She knew that she couldn't take care of this new little life but dropping him off at the hospital didn't seem like the right thing to do. She knew that she had to give him to someone who would care for him and find him a good home. The only person she trusted that much was her younger sister, who had recently married. With tear marks still lining her face, she drove up slowly to her sister's house. She walked gradually up the driveway carrying a baby and a plea for help to the front door of Danielle and George Miller's house.

Chapter 19

Tom was stunned. It didn't seem to make sense. George always seemed so loyal to the department and the mission of keeping the elite in a controlled environment. The more he found and the more he read, the more Tom realized that there was much more to George Miller than he knew. He remembered the conversation he had with George just a few short weeks ago. Tom couldn't remember what they were arguing about, but he could remember George saying, "I don't always follow the rules." Tom traced back some of the earliest documents. Many of them were memoirs that helped give him insight into what George struggled with.

<u>April 8th</u>

It's been two weeks since Danielle's sister dropped off little Kyle. The poor child doesn't really have an identity. No birth record, no social security number, no family. Legally, he doesn't exist. Danielle insisted that we name him Kyle after his mother. We had a big fight about what to do with him. This isn't what I signed up for when I asked Danielle to marry me. I told her that we needed to notify the police and get him in the proper foster care, but she insisted that we take care of him for just a few weeks. I thought it would take longer to see the stubborn side of my new wife. Neither of us knows what to do with a newborn, and we could get in serious trouble if we don't report this. For her, it is an emotional attachment. For me, everything is at risk—my career, my happiness, my life.

April 23ʳᵈ

It's been a month now with baby Kyle. I wasn't planning on dealing with babies this early in our marriage, but Danielle has fallen in love with him. To be honest, he does have a certain charm that pulls at my emotions. As cute as he is, having a baby around this early in our marriage is frustrating. Right now, his presence is not my biggest concern. The circumstances surrounding Kyle's survival were strange enough to stir my curiosity. After a tiny blood sample to confirm my suspicions, I found out today that Kyle is one of the elite. Danielle doesn't know about the blood sample or the test. In fact, she doesn't know anything about the elite. How am I going to handle this with her? I know I should report this, but I don't want to break her heart. How can I explain this to her in a way that she will understand?

Tom skimmed some of the other entries to discover that George struggled with the decision and the course of action to take that would be the least disruptive to his new marriage and not put his new career at risk. There was one other factor that affected his decision. During a time in history when classified testing was happening behind closed doors and the elite were not safe, baby Kyle had proven himself to be a survivor and George was convinced that there was a greater force orchestrating the events that led to Kyle coming into their lives.

Tom continued reading to discover that George finally did have the hard conversation with Danielle. George used all the resources he had to keep baby Kyle a secret, but just before he was three months old, George seemed to be in a hurry to make a drastic move. He took a week of vacation time and drove to Arkansas with his wife and Kyle to visit a family friend. Three left on the trip, but only two returned. George had arranged for their friend to take and raise Kyle on their farm near England, Arkansas. It was one of the largest soybean farms in the state, and it was far enough away from civilization for Kyle to grow up and remain unknown and undiscovered.

Tom sat back in his chair to ponder the journal entries he had just read. He wondered why George didn't keep Kyle longer. His answer came almost immediately as he clicked on the folder labeled 'Monitors'. Just as it was the monitors' job to profile and track the elite, someone had profiled and tracked the monitors. There was a layer in the department Tom never knew about. Within the main folder were subfolders, each with a name of one of the monitors in the department. Out of curiosity, he opened the 'Tom Marshall' first. The file contained data from his birth certificate all the way up until the day when the department was shut down. It recorded his travel, psychological profile, and habits.

Tom's childhood records, scholastic achievements, marriage, and divorce were all there. The file was more complete than his memory. It reminded him too much of the person he had been and the sacrifices he had made. Tom paused to wonder what happened to so some of his old college friends and to his ex-wife Victoria. He wished that his mom and dad could have seen that he finally did change; maybe they would have been proud. After letting his mind drift for a while, Tom refocused his attention on the screen and scrolled through the remaining monitors. It looked like everyone was there.

At first Tom thought George was responsible for profiling and tracking all the monitors, but he also had a file with his own name on it. This led Tom to believe that George was keeping this data and reporting it to someone else. George's file started soon after his trip to Arkansas, which explained why he was in such a hurry to transition Kyle to a safe place. He must have known they would find out. *Well done George,* Tom thought to himself.

Tom also noticed George's files were mysteriously missing information regarding the two trips he took each year. His mind flashed back to those times when he would question George about the trips. George would muster up a pathetic British accent and just say, "I'm off to England, Thomas." Tom remembered it so well because it bothered him that George was keeping secrets from him. Now Tom knew that George wasn't lying—not entirely anyway—and he knew why George kept it secret.

The third folder was labeled "Elite Backup Files" and, at first glance, seemed to contain a duplicate record of all the elite files up to the day that the department shut down. Tom scrolled through the files quickly, but nothing looked out of the ordinary. He was curious as to why George would keep a personal copy of the elite files instead of relying on the department server, but he dismissed it as George being thorough.

Before he knew it, midnight had snuck up on him. Tom was so excited to have finally cracked the hard drive and dig through the files that hours had passed like minutes. He yawned as if his body was trying to calm his brain enough to sleep. The puzzle pieces were finally all coming together. Tom wasn't sure what to do with all the information he had just discovered, but he knew it was time for a road trip. As he closed the laptop, he said to himself, "Off to England, Thomas," in his best British accent.

Chapter 20

The Monday morning alarm was an unwelcomed sound for Tom. He moved his arm slowly to hit the snooze button. The rest of his body felt like dead weight under the covers. He should have kept better track of time last night. The excitement of revealed mysteries overruled his need for sleep, and he was now reaping the consequences.

Arriving a little later than normal to the office wasn't a big deal as there wasn't really anyone there to report to, but Tom still felt guilty about being late. The feeling of guilt didn't deter him from stopping by the local coffee house before arriving at the deserted office building. Knowing that he needed a caffeine infusion, Tom ordered the extra-large drink and began slowly sipping the steaming beverage as he walked out the door.

Tom finally arrived at the office building and struggled to balance his coffee and laptop bag while unlocking the door. He sat down at his desk, still groggy from a long night of thinking. His eyes were heavy and shadowed by dark circles on his face. His first priority was to email Bradshaw to inform him that he was taking a small road trip to check on the status of one of the elite for a file update. Tom wrote the email as professionally as possible and explained that he would be back by the end of the week. He made sure he cached his credentials on the department server before leaving so he could remotely access the data through the VPN from the road. Then, he quickly started packing some files. He noticed that another remote connection had been established the week after Richard's capture, but he assumed George had set it up and didn't think much more about it. The caffeine was finally kicking in, and Tom began moving quickly so he could start his trip.

A last-minute glance at his email account revealed a short email response from Bradshaw approving his plan for the week and a request to let him know if any help was needed. Tom responded by thanking him for the offer and committing to an update report by the end of the week. The email message seemed like the best way to keep Bradshaw informed but avoid having to answer any detailed questions.

After packing a small suitcase and stopping by the gas station to fuel up his car, Tom started the eight-hour drive to England, Arkansas. He made a brief stop in Birmingham for lunch and finally arrived just outside Little Rock after dark. There weren't many hotels to choose from, so Tom picked the best one he could find. The long drive had made his body weary, but his mind was racing with the anticipation of meeting Kyle. After tossing and turning for what seemed like hours, Tom finally drifted off to sleep.

He awoke the next morning still unsure of what he was going to say to Kyle once he found him. The drive from the hotel to the farm where the files led him was barren and desolate. He turned down the poorly maintained dirt road that should have led him to the main driveway and followed the fence line to a wrought iron gate that was chained shut and locked with a padlock. Next to the driveway entrance was a small intercom speaker mounted on a pole. It was partially rusted and looked like it had been out in the weather for years. Tom pressed the button on the dilapidated intercom speaker box and waited for an answer. After a few seconds of silence, the speaker crackled, and a faint voice came through the static.

"Hello."

"Hi, my name is Tom Marshall. I am looking for Kyle Wagner."

"Sorry. Can't help you. No trespassing or solicitation is allowed on this property. Please turn around and leave." The voice was raspy and brash. Tom pictured a grumpy old farmer in overalls with a shotgun in one hand on the other end of the intercom system.

"No, wait. I am here on behalf of George Miller…"

The speaker was silent. Tom sat for a minute hoping to again here a voice so he could explain the reason for his visit. He tried pushing the button again, but nothing happened. Tom grabbed his jacket and stepped out of his car. He walked to the gate, which had two very large "No Trespassing" signs on it. He tried to look down the road to see if there was a house in view. The dirt driveway inclined up a hill and turned to the left, making it impossible to see anything but dirt and grass.

Confident that the farm residents had underestimated his resolve, Tom placed his hands on the top of the gate and prepared to climb over. He was almost halfway up when he saw an object in the sky falling toward him. The sun was blinding his view, but he could tell that it was rectangular, and it was coming straight at him. Tom jumped down off the gate and covered his face with his arm just before the flying object hit the gate with tremendous force, making the chain rattle. A cloud of dust engulfed the area. Tom squinted to avoid getting dust in his eyes and looked to see the large projectile laying on the ground beside his car. It was a bale of hay launched from somewhere over the hill on the other side of the fence.

Unsure of his next move, Tom stood still and silent for a few minutes. Since the residents didn't show any interest in talking over the intercom anymore, and they clearly didn't approve of his attempt to climb the fence, Tom opted for a more direct approach. He walked up to the front of the gate and shouted as loud as he could.

"My name is Tom Marshall. George was my friend, but he's dead now. His wife entrusted me with the information about Kyle. I need to talk to him. I promise I am not going to hurt anyone."

Silence.

"I drove a long way to see Kyle, and I'm not leaving until I do," he shouted.

Minutes passed. Without warning the intercom speaker crackled. He walked back over to the pole it was mounted on and bent down to try to hear a voice, but there was only static. He pushed the button, but no one responded. He stood up straight and heard a sound in the distance behind him. Suddenly, he felt a sharp pain just under his left shoulder blade. Tom reached behind his back but then became dizzy. The world started to spin in his vision and then everything became blurry. His legs gave out, and he fell to the ground. He blinked trying to regain his senses, but his eyelids moved slowly. Suddenly, everything went black.

Chapter 21

Tom opened his eyes to discover that he was lying on a twin-size bed in a small bedroom. The furnishings were outdated, mostly centered around an old-fashioned, country-style décor. The room looked old and worn. He had been stripped of his jacket, as well as the contents of his pockets, and was left with only a dull headache. He attempted to stand to his feet, but his legs were still weak. His head was heavy and groggy. The floor creaked, and he heard footsteps approach the bedroom door. The door opened, and an older black man walked through. He was dressed in a stained white t-shirt, overalls, and worn boots. On top of his head was an old rugged red baseball cap that was faded and stained.

"Good afternoon, Mr. Marshall."

"Tranquilizer dart?" Tom said rubbing the back of his neck to clear the fog in his head.

"I'm afraid so; compliments to your friend George Miller. I'm sorry about that, but we have gone to some pretty extreme measures to keep Kyle safe from the world and from a government that might exploit him."

"Well, your aim is pretty good."

"Thanks. Kyle and I train quite a bit when we're waiting for the crop to come in."

"So, you know who I am. I didn't get your name."

"Walter Evans. I took the liberty of glancing through the folders in your bag to make sure your story checked out. Mind telling me why you're here?"

"I read the file George kept on Kyle. I assume you and your wife are the ones who took Kyle in when he was a baby."

"Yes, my wife Mary died a few years ago. Now it's just me and Kyle."

"I'm sorry to hear about your wife. George and I worked together. I came here to tell you that he's gone. I also wanted to see the miracle boy that I read so much about."

"He's not much of a boy anymore," Walter said. "He'll be thirty-six next month." Walter stopped to reflect on the news of George's death. His expression became sad. He looked down toward the floor and paused before his next words.

"George and I grew up together. After high school, he went on to bigger and better things while I moved out here, got married, and took over my uncle's farm. Still, we kept in touch as much as possible. Mary and I couldn't have any kids of our own, so when George called me and asked me to help with Kyle, we didn't hesitate. George said that he was special and, oh my, did we find that out for ourselves. That was so long ago. We did the best we could with him. George would come over twice a year to check up on us and make sure everything was going okay."

"I would like to talk to him if that's alright."

"Sure. You slept through lunch and most of the afternoon. Kyle is almost done making supper, so why don't you freshen up and let's talk over a warm meal."

Walter's suggestion sounded like a great idea. After hearing that he had missed lunch, Tom felt hungry. As Walter left the room, Tom stumbled to the hall bathroom to splash some cold water on his face. The smell of fresh baked bread filled the hallway and made his stomach growl.

It wasn't hard for Tom to find the kitchen. The house was small, and the smell led him straight to his destination. He glanced out every window to see nothing but trees and farmland. As he walked into the kitchen, he noticed a tall, muscular black man standing over the outdated white stove. Tom knew instantly that it was Kyle. Tom stopped in the doorway to the kitchen as Kyle turned and extended his hand.

"Good afternoon, Mr. Marshall."

His voice was deep and strong. As they shook hands, his grip was tight but not painful. Tom was keenly aware that Kyle could have crushed his hand if he wanted to. He was wearing blue jeans and a red flannel shirt with the sleeves rolled up—just like George used to wear his dress shirts. Although his shirt was large enough to be loose fitting, it couldn't hide the muscles that were bulging all over his arms and torso. Kyle was impressive to say the least.

Knowing that they had much to talk about, Walter and Kyle got straight to the point as everyone sat down to eat. Walter said a prayer to bless the food and started right in with a question.

"What happened to George?"

"Someone broke into his house. He kept an external hard drive with information about Kyle, files on all the monitors, and a backup copy of all the files on the elite. My guess is that someone found out that he was hiding something, and they were pretty desperate to find it. I don't know if George came home unexpectedly and surprised them or if he was already in the house when they got there. According to Danielle, they roughed him up pretty bad."

"So, George entrusted you with this before he died?"

"No, actually. Danielle knew about the hard drive but didn't know what was on it. George had it pretty well protected. She thought that whoever broke into their house and killed George was after the information. She found him on the floor when she got home, and he died in her arms. After that, she didn't want anything to do with the part of his life that he couldn't share with her."

"Are Danielle and the kids okay?"

"Yes. I saw them at the funeral. They were understandably shaken up at first, but they seemed to be handling it well."

Kyle remained silent for most of the dinner. He had started with heaping mounds of vegetables but was steadily shrinking the piles. Everything on the plate was fresh. If they didn't grow and raise it there, it must have come from another farm close by. There was so much Tom wanted to ask Walter and Kyle, but the conversation about George made him remember his consistent coaching to focus more on the relationship and less on business. He decided to probe a bit more into the history of the friendship between George and Walter.

"Tell me more about your relationship with George."

"George and I were neighbors when we were kids. We grew up in the same neighborhood, went to the same school, and played basketball on the street right outside our houses. He was always a good friend to me. Still, I was a bit surprised when he called me about Kyle. I asked him why he called me. I thought surely he had made new friends that he could trust and that were closer to his home in Atlanta. I'll never forget what he told me. He said 'Walt, the true test of character is consistency over time.' Trust was a hard thing for George early in his years."

Tom was fascinated by the backstory of their friendship. Walter continued to tell stories as they ate. He had a sharp memory for someone his age. He gave Tom insight into some of the great times and some of the dark times in George's life. The evening passed quickly and before they knew it, the chill of night covered the land. Tom helped Walter and Kyle clean up after dinner and accepted their invitation to stay for a few days.

As the kitchen chores came to a close, Walter and Kyle both retired to their rooms for the evening. Having slept most of the day, Tom stayed up reading until his eyelids became heavy and his body could resist the warmth of the soft blanket no more.

Chapter 22

Tom woke to the sound of roosters breaking through the silence of his slumber. The sun was rising over the ridge shedding a small beam of light on the wall just above his head. He could hear a fire rustling from the living room, so he knew someone was already awake. The smell of aged wood filled the air as Tom took a deep breath and sat up in the bed.

Tom slid his legs out of the warm covers and planted his feet on the cold floor. He peered out the window to get a better view of the landscape. The farmhouse sat on an acre of land with trees and grass just as if it were in a regular neighborhood. To the east was a small ridge and where Tom assumed his car was still sitting at the front gate. To the west he could see a large shed where he figured most of the farm equipment was stored. The rest of the land he could see was barren farmland covered with spots of snow and ice.

At the foot of the bed, Tom noticed that someone had been kind enough to bring in his suitcase from the car. After a shower and a change of clothes, he walked to the living room where Kyle and Walter were sitting and enjoying a cup of coffee.

"Good morning, Mr. Marshall," Kyle said, looking up from the raised fireplace hearth where he was seated. Walter occupied a rocking chair on the other side of the fireplace. The whole living room smelled like bacon mixed with a scent of smoke from the fire.

"Good morning. Please call me Tom."

"Okay," Kyle said as he stood, "can I get you some coffee?"

"That would be great. Thank you."

Tom sat on the couch across from the fireplace as Kyle came back in the room, handed him a steaming mug, and sat back down near the fireplace. There were a few minutes of silence as he sipped the hot coffee.

"According to the news, there's going to be an ice storm this afternoon," Walter said. "You're welcome to stay to wait out the weather until it is safe to drive."

"Thanks. If you're sure it's okay, I will. I've never really been on a farm this big before."

"Well then," Walter replied, "Kyle will show you around after breakfast. There's not much to see in the way of crops right now. We're waiting until spring to plant."

"That sounds great, Walter. Thanks for your hospitality. I do need to hop online and check on some things while I'm here."

"You'll have to drive into town for that," Walter said with a grin. Tom checked his phone to verify Walter's response.

"Yep, no signal."

"There's a small public library on Taylor Street in town where you can get internet access. It doesn't open until 10:00. Don't expect it to be fast, but it will be your best option. We're not very high-tech around these parts."

Tom smiled in acknowledgement and made small talk while they all finished their coffee. After breakfast, Kyle gave Tom a tour of the farm.

"I would have expected to see more tractors and machinery," Tom said as they walked down a frozen tundra path that ran between two of the fields.

"We still do a lot the old-fashioned way," Kyle said with a smile, "tilling and plowing helps keep me in shape."

"If you don't mind me asking, have you ever had any issues with your strength?"

"What do you mean issues?"

"Breaking faucet handles, doorknobs, anything like that?"

"Nothing like that. I guess I just don't know any different."

"That make sense," Tom replied as they continued walking. "You're the only elite who has grown up with these abilities."

"Elite?"

"Yes. It's what we call people like you."

"That sounds fancy," Kyle said sarcastically.

"It is." Tom replied. "You should feel honored."

"Look at me. I've been on this farm my whole life. I wear faded jeans, boots, and flannel shirts. I cut my own hair. I catch and grow my own food. There's nothing about me that is 'elite'."

"There's a whole big world of ordinary people out there. Trust me, you are special. The 'elite' label fits you perfectly."

"Do the other elite break faucet handles and doorknobs?" Kyle asked.

Tom smirked. "Sometimes."

"Tell me about them."

"Most of the elite don't even realize they are special."

"George told me about the restrainer chip. I asked him once if there were others like me. He told me there were, but they just didn't know it."

"For the most part, he was right. Last year two of the elite broke their restrainer chips and quickly discovered they had a strength they had never felt before."

"What happened to them?"

"One of them made some bad decisions and took a dark road. The other one dealt with some tough issues, but he is doing fine now. In fact, I would consider him a friend."

Kyle listened intently as Tom told him about Jacob and Christina. He didn't feel comfortable enough sharing all the details about the incidents with Richard and Jacob, but he shared enough of the story to satisfy Kyle's curiosity.

"They sound like good people," Kyle said.

"They are. They have taught me a lot about life."

"And Jacob doesn't have a restrainer chip anymore?"

"No. I'm supposed to schedule him to get another one, but he isn't sure that is the right choice."

"Do you think it's the right choice?" Kyle asked.

"I don't know. What would you tell him?"

"I have learned that when something special has been given to you, it is meant to be used," Kyle said.

Tom was puzzled. "Say more."

"There was one time I got sick. Miss Mary made me stay in bed to rest and I got better, but I could feel the energy building up inside of me and had to get it out. It was about the same time we needed to dig a drainage ditch on the south side of the farm. Mr. Walter said he had never seen anyone dig a ditch so fast. It felt so good to work out the energy."

"Fascinating. So, you don't think people with special abilities should be restrained?"

"You made it sound like there were already too many ordinary people in the world," Kyle said with a smile. "It may not be a bad idea to have a few 'elite' folks around to mix it up."

"George made the right decision with you, Kyle."

Looking down at his watch, Kyle continued, "You should probably get into town if you want to be back before the storm hits."

"Thanks, Kyle."

Although it was still early in the day, Tom could feel the temperature dropping. They walked back to the house where Tom grabbed an extra jacket. Walter gave him some brief directions on how to get to the town library and sent him on his way. The conversation with Kyle about the ethics of the restrainer chip circulated in his head as he drove. He was hoping to get more time later to discuss the subject with Kyle.

Chapter 23

After getting lost twice, I finally found the public library in the small town of England, Arkansas. Walter was correct about the speed of the internet connection, but after a few attempts, I successfully logged in to the remote server and downloaded email. While waiting for the email, my phone latched on to a cellular signal and a voicemail notification grabbed my attention. I hated missing calls, but not having any cellular service for the past day made it unavoidable. As I checked my phone, I found two messages and played them back in order.

"Tom. This is Robert. We wanted to talk to you about Jacob. He's probably too stubborn to tell you himself, but Suzanna and I are a bit concerned. The past few days he has had some headaches. At first it wasn't out of the ordinary, but they are getting more frequent and sometimes they get bad. He tried convincing us that it's no big deal, but you can understand why Suzanna, Christina, and I are all a little worried. He probably won't like the fact that we called you about this,

129

but… we just want to make sure he is okay. Please call me when you can. Thanks."

The second message was from Jacob and was much more mysterious. As Robert predicted, Jacob made no mention of any headaches.

"Hey Tom. It's Jacob. Riley finally opened up and told us about her abduction. I think there's something happening behind the scenes, and I'd like you to hear her story firsthand as soon as you get the chance. Let me know when we can meet. Thanks."

Robert's call and Jacob's message reinforced my decision to drive back home as soon as the storm passed.

Tom Marshall Monitor Log Personal File BGEN3113
End of Record

Tom arrived back on the farm before sunset and told Kyle and Walter that he would need to leave first thing in the morning.

"Is everything okay?" Kyle asked.

"I'm not sure yet," Tom responded, "I got some concerning voicemails from the Monroes, and I think there may be some trouble brewing back home. They are the only true family I've ever known, and if I can help them in any way, then I should be there for them."

Just as Walter predicted, the ice storm blew through that night, leaving a glossy white coat on the landscape.

It was Friday morning. Tom packed his suitcase before joining Kyle and Walter for breakfast. His plan for the lonely drive home took an unexpected turn when he sat down at the kitchen table.

"Good morning, Tom."

"Good morning, Kyle."

"I would like to ask a favor of you if you don't mind."

"Sure," Tom said.

"I would like to go back to Atlanta with you."

His request caught Tom off guard. Kyle had never traveled anywhere or even been off the farm. Without an identity, his travel options were limited. Walter sat across from Tom at the table and stayed silent. Tom glanced at him as he gave an approving nod.

"It's okay with me if it's okay with Walter," Tom replied, trying to ensure he interpreted Walter's reaction correctly. They both looked back at Kyle as he continued.

"I've been thinking a lot about what you said when we talked about the Monroe family and, well, it would be nice to meet someone like me and be able to talk. Besides, it sounds like there may be trouble coming, and I think I can help."

"Kyle, you are welcome to come stay with me for a while, but I'm not going to drag you into a fight. That would be taking advantage of your abilities, and I don't want you to feel obligated."

"With all due respect, Mr. Marshall, I am here because George Miller saved my life. He thought I could use these gifts to help someone someday who really needed me. I think today is a good day to start down the path of finding out if he was right."

It was clear that Kyle had thought about this, and his mind was set. It was also clear that Kyle and Walter had discussed it and there was no changing his mind. With that, Tom relented.

"I would be happy to take you back with me."

"I'd also like to see Mrs. Miller to offer my condolences."

"I'm sure we can arrange that."

The excitement beamed from Kyle's face as he politely excused himself from the kitchen to go pack a bag for the trip.

Tom could hear him down the hall whispering to himself as he packed. He then turned to Walter to reassure him that Kyle would be in good hands.

"I'll take good care of him, Walter."

"I know you will," he said with a grin, "and even if you don't, believe me, Kyle can take care of himself."

"I'm sure he can, Walter."

Chapter 24

The drive home seemed much faster to Tom than the drive to Arkansas he made early that week. Kyle had warmed up to him and was fully engaged in their conversation.

Naturally, Kyle had a lot of questions about his own origins. Tom recounted the story of Kyle's mom, the clinic, and the nurse who saved his life to the best of his memory. When they stopped for a break, Tom retrieved all of George's old files on his laptop and let Kyle read them for himself. It was difficult for Tom to see such a big, strong man reading with tears swelling up in his eyes and running down his cheeks.

Kyle was curious to hear more about the other elite. He asked a lot of questions that Tom didn't have answers for. The exchange of questions was mutual since Tom wanted to hear more about how Kyle grew up and how Walter and Mary dealt with his abilities. The more Tom pieced together what he had read in George's files and what Kyle told him, the more he learned about George's real feelings concerning the elite.

While the government leadership was in the early stages of researching and developing ways to control the elite, George was forced into a different thought process when baby Kyle showed up at his doorstep. During one of his semi-annual visits to Arkansas, Kyle asked George why he was the only one not restrained by the chip. George believed that the focused attempt to restrain and control the supernatural abilities of the elite is what led to the death of so many young elite, including John and Julie. He was convinced that if the elite were allowed to develop naturally—without being probed and tested—their bodies and brains would grow to support their extraordinary abilities.

The key missing ingredient was making sure that their bodies got what they needed regarding nutrition and exercise. Together, George and Walter had figured out the nutrient mix that Kyle needed to satisfy his body as it adapted to a higher level of strength than the average person. Their testing strategy was not well organized, but the final result was obviously successful. Tom wasn't sure George's theory would work for every elite, but there was a viable example sitting in the car right next to him.

Kyle's very existence made Tom question the motives of his government leadership. He had always been told that the restraining chips and close monitoring of each elite were for their own safety and the security of society. He was convinced that without the restrainer chip, the elite would not survive. George knew otherwise. It made sense to him now why George was not in any hurry to reimplant Jacob's chip; he had living proof that the elite can survive without it.

With George's oversight and Walter and Mary's care, Kyle had learned to handle his ability. He learned the limits of his strength and how to set thresholds for how much force he applied when giving a hug, shaking a hand, or pulling weeds in Mary's garden. He managed his own biological adrenaline levels by understanding when he could just sit and relax and when he had to go outside and burn off energy. He also understood when his body needed a jolt of nutrients.

Tom was convinced that Kyle was more than just George's alternative experiment. He was George's backup plan. Despite the protocols and procedures that had been developed, if there was ever an incident with the elite, George had a secret weapon hidden on a soybean farm in Arkansas.

Kyle explained to Tom how George set him up with specific training exercises to sharpen his skills and use his abilities to the greatest potential should the need arise. He didn't go into a lot of details regarding the training, but Tom knew from firsthand experience that Kyle could launch a hay bale from two hundred yards away and hit his target with precision and accuracy.

Tom wondered why George didn't consider asking Kyle to help capture Richard. Perhaps George wasn't ready to expose his secret weapon for fear of retribution from the authorities, or perhaps he didn't feel comfortable with General Corbin and his men's military presence during the mission. Although Tom didn't know the reason, he was sure that George had a good one. It made Tom recognize that, as keeper of this information now, he needed to be cautious about when and where to ask Kyle for help.

Tom's thoughts were interrupted as Kyle finished reading a file and attempted to make conversation. It was obvious he didn't have much practice with social skills.

"What are you afraid of, Mr. Marshall?"

The question came out of the blue and created a bit of an awkward pause.

"Well, I guess I don't think about my fears much. I guess I'm afraid of being unforgiven for all the wrong I have done. Sometimes I feel like it's not fair that I didn't have to endure the consequences of my actions, but at the same time, I fear those consequences."

Kyle pondered. Tom, also being inexperienced at deep conversation, tossed the question back at Kyle.

"What are you afraid of?"

"Not being who I am supposed to be. Given the circumstances surrounding my birth, the fact that I survived at all is a miracle. Now I have all these abilities and I have trained to control them, but I am not using them to help anyone. That's why I asked to come."

It was clear that Kyle had thought about his identity a lot while isolated from society on the farm. As Tom thought more about Kyle's answer, it made him realize his own identity insecurities.

"I guess on some level, we are all afraid of not fulfilling our purpose," Tom said, almost to himself.

The reassurance that he was not alone in dealing with purpose brought a small grin to Kyle's face and ended the conversation. Kyle returned to staring out the window admiring scenery that he had never witnessed before.

Chapter 25

"That would be great sweetheart, and don't forget the lettuce," she paused. "I love you, too. See you soon."

Christina put the phone down on the kitchen counter as Riley handed her another dish. Christina and Riley bonded quickly and found that some of their best conversations happened while washing the dishes together. Jacob was surprised at how fast Riley embraced them as her new family. There were still days when Riley spent a lot of time in her room dealing with the past and processing the changes with her environment. Even on the bad days, she was still a very pleasant addition to their home. Riley was grateful to Jacob and Christina for letting her stay with them, and she was intentional about offering a helping hand wherever she could.

"I assume that was Jake."

"Well, I doubt if you'll ever hear me tell another man that I love him over the phone," Christina said with a smile. "He'll be leaving work in about thirty minutes, and he's stopping by the store for me on the way home to grab what we need for dinner tonight."

"He's a good guy."

"Yes, he is. There would be a huge void in my life without Jacob. You are an attractive young lady, Riley. One day, you'll find someone special too."

"Oh, I'm not into that yet, trust me. I do envy the life you have though; loving husband, caring in-laws, a stable home."

"Well, it's not without some trials and struggles," Christina said knocking on the arm of her wheelchair, "but you are right, my life is blessed. I don't take that for granted."

"Can I tell you a secret?"

"Of course, you can. You're family now."

"I was ready for it all to end the day Tom caught up to me. I just felt like I had nothing to live for. I had nowhere to go and no one to turn to..."

Riley stopped and looked down at her feet. The tears were swelling in her eyes, and she was struggling to hold them back. She didn't like exposing herself emotionally to anyone. She had never said that out loud before. The transparency made her feel vulnerable, but she felt comfortable with Christina. Christina gently reached over and put her hand on top of Riley's hand.

"It's okay Riley. You've been through a lot lately. No one would judge you for those feelings," Christina said with a warm smile. Riley grinned and looked up at Christina. Her eyes were flooded, and red splotches had developed on her face.

"You and Jake and Tom, you saved my life."

"Well, I don't think any of us want to take all that credit. You are a great person, Riley, and I am so glad you are here with us. You've been a great help and a huge encouragement to us."

"I guess we'll call it even then," Riley said, unable to hold back the single stream of tears that came down her left cheek. She wiped her face with the back of her hand and smiled.

"Can I tell you a secret?" Christina asked maintaining her grin.

"Sure," Riley said.

"He hates it when you call him Jake."

Riley smiled so big that she exposed the dimples on her splotchy cheeks.

"I know," she said.

Riley handed Christina the last plate for drying and drained the sink of the soapy water. She still had something on her mind but wasn't sure how to ask.

"Christina, do you trust me?"

"Of course, I do."

"There's something I want to do. I feel like I need to do it. Not because I have to, but because I really want to. Would you let me?"

"It's not dangerous, is it?"

"No," she said as she paused for a moment. "Those men who kidnapped me told me I could heal someone, and they were going to make me do it. Then, Tom told me about the elite and how he had been watching over me my whole life."

Christina was a little perplexed, not sure of what Riley was trying to say, but she let her continue anyway.

"Do you think it's true?"

"I know that there are people out there with special abilities. I know Jacob is extraordinarily strong, and I know his sister Julie had the ability to heal people so, yes, I do believe that you could be one of those special people who have supernatural abilities."

"I want to try it."

"Umm.... okay. You're not going to cut me or anything, are you?"

"No," Riley said with a grin. Although Christina was partially joking with her last question, she was relieved to hear Riley's answer.

"But I do want to try healing you. I want to see you walk again."

Christina was shocked. "Oh, Riley. I don't know. That is a pretty big deal. The doctors said that there was so much damage and..."

"Please, Christina. Please let me try."

"I'm sorry Riley, I just can't let you do that." Christina paused as the thought sunk into her mind. "It's too much to hope for. It's too big of a task. The accident completely severed my spinal cord. I am so grateful for your tender heart, but..."

"I have to know if it works," Riley interrupted, "I can finally repay you for all you've done for me."

"Riley, I don't need you to repay us. We took you in because we wanted to. We're supposed to help each other. That's what God tells us to do."

"Then prove it and let me try to help you."

Christina paused knowing that she was trapped with her own words. The internal struggle was challenging her mind. She wanted to walk again so much. The thought of walking to the front door to greet Jacob with a kiss when he came home from work like she used to do every day lifted her spirit. At the same time, she was also afraid that her hopes could be crushed or that it could prove too much for Riley to handle. The thoughts rushed through her head in a split second. Riley was looking at her, intently waiting for a response.

"Ok. But promise me if something doesn't feel right, we'll stop right away."

"Pinky promise," Riley said with a new gleam of hope in her eyes.

Christina threw the dishtowel onto the kitchen counter and maneuvered her wheelchair into the master bedroom with Riley following closely behind her. Riley helped her climb onto the bed.

Christina laid stomach down on the bed and lifted her shirt to expose her back.

"That was quite the little workout," Christina said. "Are you sure you want to try this?"

"Absolutely."

Riley stood next to the foot of the bed and reached out, putting both hands on Christina's bare back. Christina flinched as Riley's cold hands touched her warm skin. In her mind, Riley pictured the severed spinal cord. She pretended to see the tissue and bone coming back together again. She felt the warmth of Christina's back on the palms of her hands.

Christina lay perfectly still. She too felt the increasing warmth of Riley's touch on her back. They were both silent. They held their positions for several minutes with their eyes closed. Christina prayed without speaking. She prayed for healing, but also prayed for a grateful heart if God chose not to heal her.

Suddenly, Christina felt her toes tingling. She had phantom feelings in the past, so she couldn't tell if it was real or not. She couldn't see her toes from the position she was in, but she couldn't fight the feeling that she had to wiggle them. Riley gasped.

"What's wrong," Christina asked, "what is it?"

"Your toes moved," Riley exclaimed, not wanting to remove her hands from her back. She almost couldn't believe her eyes. "Try moving your feet."

144

Christina lay still as the seconds passed.

"Are you trying?"

"Yes, are they moving?"

"Not yet, keep trying."

Riley was starting to become discouraged. She thought maybe the initial excitement distracted her, so she focused on Christina's back. After a few seconds, she turned to look at Christina's feet. Suddenly the right foot shifted, and the left foot moved.

"It's working Christina, it's working."

Christina began weeping as the warm spot on her back started moving down her legs. She could feel the edge of the bed rubbing against her feet. Riley started to feel tired, but she kept pressing. She was afraid to let go. Christina's silent prayer became an audible praise as she felt sensations in her legs that had only existed in her memory. Tears welled up in Riley's eyes as Christina started singing the same song they heard in church that previous Sunday.

Riley could feel her body weaken, but it wasn't overwhelming. She kept her hands on Christina's back and listened to Christina praise God in the middle of the miracle. As she sang, Christina's feet moved steady with the beat. A small tear dripped from Riley's cheek onto her arm and rolled toward her hand. The feeling made her instinctively lift her hand to wipe her arm.

Christina rolled over onto her back. The amazement was evident in her eyes. The dead weight of her legs suddenly felt like they were alive again. Riley felt physically drained and knelt by the foot of the bed.

"Are you okay?" Christina asked as her hand reached for Riley.

"Yes," she answered with a smile on her face and tears in her eyes. "It worked. It really worked."

"Riley, this is amazing. You're amazing. God is amazing. I just don't know what else to say. I'm so grateful. I'm…"

"Rambling," Riley interrupted. "You're rambling. Now let's see if you can do more than just wiggle those feet. Time for both of us to stand up. You do remember how to walk, don't you?"

"There's one way to find out."

Almost an hour later, Jacob entered the house with two bags of groceries. As he walked through the front door, he was stopped by Riley, who was smiling and crying at the same time.

"Riley, are you okay? What's wrong?" Jacob asked.

"Stay right there, Jake," she continued, "I'll take those bags off your hands."

Jacob handed her the bags and stayed in the doorway without a clue of what was happening. Then movement from the hallway grabbed his attention, and he glanced over to see his wife walking gingerly toward him. His instinct was to go to her, but he was stopped by her voice.

"No. You stay right where you are," Christina said, stammering a little but making good progress walking toward Jacob. "It's been too long since I've been able to walk to the front door to greet you when you came home."

Jacob was speechless. His eyes filled with tears, and his jaw dropped slightly. He couldn't believe what he was seeing. Christina took small steps toward him. Her hand kept contact with the wall to stabilize her balance. Her eyes were locked onto his. He couldn't hold back his excitement any longer. As she approached, despite his mandate to not move, he took the two steps required to meet her and immediately joined his lips to hers. He held her tight as they embraced. Christina looked at Riley, who was standing in the doorway to the kitchen, and simply mouthed the words "thank you".

Chapter 26

Tom and Kyle arrived in Atlanta by late evening. He called Danielle and arranged a brief meeting in a secluded local café to ensure her safety. She was so anxious to see Kyle that she arrived before they did. Tom parked across the street and stayed in the car to give them some privacy. He could see the tears in her eyes as she watched Kyle get out of the car and walk across the street. Their embrace was sweet and tender. It was like watching a mother reconnecting with her long-lost son. They sat inside the café and talked for an hour, sometimes laughing, and sometimes crying. Tom sat in the car watching through the window, and consistently checking to make sure no one else was watching. He had built a career based on watching others from a distance, so the circumstance was more familiar than boring.

They left the café arm in arm. Danielle wrote something on a small piece of paper and gave it to Kyle. He folded the paper and placed it in his pocket. They embraced once more before Kyle walked back to the car. Tom watched Danielle as she made eye contact with him and expressed her appreciation with a smile. He nodded to acknowledge her gratitude as Kyle got in the car. They waited until she left to ensure she was safe. Kyle didn't say much the rest of the way back home. Tom never asked him about the conversation, but he did get the sense that the reunion helped bring closure to both of their lives.

After the long drive and emotional reunion, Kyle slept soundly on Tom's couch and was wide awake at 7:00am. He attempted to quietly make breakfast for Tom and himself using the scarcely stocked kitchen pantry. As much as he tried to stay quiet, Kyle was unfamiliar with the kitchen layout and had to open and close several cabinet doors and drawers to find what he needed. The open floor plan of Tom's house made it feel larger than it was but offered no insulation from the clattering of pots and pans. The noise woke Tom, who walked in the living room still half-asleep.

"Good morning," Kyle said with a big smile.

"Good morning. You certainly are the morning person, aren't you?"

"Yes sir. I normally get up at six, so I guess with the time difference, it's about right."

"Were you comfortable last night?"

"Yes. I slept just fine, thank you."

"I've been using the spare room as a home office, but I'll get it cleaned out so you can have a room for yourself. Is that coffee?"

"Yes. I did what I could with what you had."

"It's great. Thanks, Kyle. Coffee first, and then we need to go visit the Monroes."

Tom got dressed and ate breakfast with Kyle before calling Jacob to ensure they were out of bed already. Jacob answered the phone immediately after the first ring.

"Good morning, Tom. Oh yes, we are all up," Jacob said as he watched Christina walk around their small kitchen. "Please come on over. There's something we would like you to see. Mom and Dad are coming over too."

Tom and Kyle arrived mid-morning to find Jacob sipping coffee on the porch steps. Tom's mind was focused on finally hearing Riley's story. He didn't even notice that the handicap ramp was gone.

"Good morning, Jacob. I'd like you to meet Kyle. You two have a lot in common."

Kyle smiled and stretched out his hand to greet Jacob. They exchanged a firm handshake before Jacob invited them both inside. Robert and Suzanna had already arrived and were waiting in the living room. Kyle introduced himself to Robert and Suzanna before taking a seat in the rocking chair next to the fireplace. Tom shook Robert's hand and Suzanna greeted him with a hug before they sat down on the couch. Tom noticed that Suzanna was beaming with excitement as she sat next to her husband and grabbed his hand.

"Are you ready?" Jacob asked.

"Ready for what?" Tom replied.

"Christina, come on out sweetheart."

Christina emerged from the hallway and walked straight over to Kyle to shake his hand.

"It's nice to meet you, Kyle. Tom, welcome back to our home. Can I get you guys any coffee or anything?"

Tom was shocked.

"Christina, what happened?"

"The young lady you left in our care turned out to be a little miracle worker," Christina said as Riley appeared from the hallway. She glanced at Kyle who smiled and nodded at her. She smiled back and then turned to see Tom's reaction. A dozen questions filled Tom's head.

"Riley, you did this?"

"Yes sir," she replied.

"How did you know what to do?"

"That's what I wanted to talk to you about, Mr. Marshall." Riley said as she pulled in a chair from the dining table to sit down. "It was just after Christmas. I was still on break from school and walking down to the grocery store to pick up some food for dinner. Suddenly, this kid comes up behind me and says my name like he knows me. My school is pretty big, so I thought maybe he knew me from there, but I didn't recognize him at all. He said he worked for someone who was looking for people like me and asked if I wanted a job. There was another boy with him about the same age. He was a young black guy, but he didn't say anything."

"Did you get their names or remember anything specific about their appearance, like a tattoo or something?" Tom asked.

"He said his name was Jeremy. The other one didn't say anything. He just stood there watching. Jeremy was smaller than me with pale skin and lots of pimples on his cheeks. He had a creepy smile too. I told him I wasn't interested in a job and tried to walk away. I felt him grab me at my waist, and then I felt this moist cloth on my face. I tried to scream, but then I blacked out."

"What do you remember next?"

"I woke up tied to a chair in a room about the size of a classroom at my school. It was dimly lit with no windows and smelled musty. I was so scared that I started screaming for help. That is when I saw Jeremy again. He came in the room and told me to calm down. He said all I had to do was one thing, and then they would let me go."

Everyone in the room was captivated by Riley's story. She continued while tears started streaming from her eyes.

"He left the room and came back a few minutes later holding a kitten. He said the kitten had a broken leg, and that I had the power to heal it. All I had to do was try. My mind was still foggy. I kept thinking this was a really bad dream. I was so scared that my whole body was shaking. He set the kitten in my lap and untied my hands, but I was too scared to touch it. It just sat there whimpering in my lap. Suddenly, there was a lot of yelling and commotion going on down the hallway outside the room. Jeremy ran out of the room, and I heard somebody yell, "Get them!"

Chapter 27

The tears were flowing more heavily as Tom interrupted, "Riley, you don't have to go on if it's too painful." She paused to regain her composure.

"No, I need to finish. I sat there feeling paralyzed for a minute, and then I grabbed the kitten, stood up, and ran out the door. I heard yelling to my right, so I ran in the other direction with the whimpering kitten still in my arms. I saw a door with an exit sign on it and ran as fast as I could. I rushed through the doorway and ran into this other kid wearing a black hooded jacket. We both fell to the ground. I knew he was as shocked and scared as I was. He grabbed my arm, told me to run, and not look back. We ran for a long time and hid under a highway overpass that runs through the center of downtown. It wasn't until then that I knew I wasn't in Charlotte anymore."

"I asked him where we were. He said Atlanta. Then he told me to get rid of the kitten or they would hear it. He said, 'You can't let them get you again.'"

"I told him I couldn't just leave it with a broken leg. He took the kitten from me and held on to its broken leg for a minute. Then it stopped whining. As he put the kitten down, it ran away. I asked him who he was and how he did that."

"He said his name was Joshua, and that he could heal people. I looked at him in disbelief. I could tell he was trying to be strong, but tears swelled in his eyes as he spoke. I asked him what they did to him, and he told me his story."

"He said they took him and his mom. They tied him to a chair in a room just like they did to me. He told me they held this device up to the back of his neck. He felt something pop like a chiropractor cracked his back and he passed out. He said when he woke up, they brought him a kitten with a broken leg, just like they did to me. They kept insisting that he could heal the kitten. He was hesitant at first, but it didn't take long for him to get so desperate to leave that he had to try something. He told me he didn't know what to do. He tried talking to the kitten and holding it in different positions, but nothing worked. Then he said he held the broken leg and concentrated real hard. At first nothing happened, but then he said he felt a strange warmth in his hand and the kitten's leg got better.

"When I asked him about his mom, he couldn't hold back the tears any longer. He said they brought him to a room where his mom was tied up in a chair. She had tape over her mouth. He said there was so much fear in her eyes. One guy walked up to her with a big army knife and cut her arm. Then the guy told him to

156

heal her. He told me he was so scared. He said he put his hand right on the cut, closed his eyes, and held it there for a minute. When he lifted his hand, he was shocked to see the cut was gone. They kept hurting her worse and worse and after each time, they told him to heal her. He said it got easier for him, but with each cut, it took longer because they kept cutting deeper."

"He paused for a long time. I could tell that the situation got much worse, but it was too painful for him to recall. I told him I didn't need to hear any more, and we sat in silence for a few minutes. He told me he had been there for several days. He also said there were more like us there. Some had been taken, but others seemed to want to be there. He told me he and one of the other guys named Alan planned an escape, but it didn't work out like they thought it would, so they split up. That's when he ran into me."

Christina left the room to retrieve a box of tissues for Riley as Tom interjected, "I'm so sorry, Riley. That must have been terrible." He paused. "What you did was very brave. This is going to help me figure all this out, and I'm going to make sure they don't come back to hurt you again."

"Thank you, Mr. Marshall," Riley said as she took a deep breath.

"Do you know what happened to Joshua after that?" Tom asked.

"No sir. After that, he gave me a fifty-dollar bill and told me to go to the bus station on Forsyth Street. He told me to get as far away from there as possible. I asked him what he was going to do. He just said he was going to see some old friends. I went to the bus station just like he told me to. I never saw him again. When I got back home, I knew Grammy would be worried, so I ran home as fast as I could, but when I found her…"

Riley's soft tears became sobbing. An awkward sadness filled the room. No one knew exactly what to say. Christina entered the room with a full box of tissue.

"That's enough, Riley," Tom said breaking the silence. He made eye contact with Christina and she knew exactly what to do. "Thank you for what you have shared, but I think that's enough for today."

Riley nodded in agreement.

"Come on Riley, let's go get you freshened up," Christina said as she took Riley's hand and led her to the bathroom.

"What do you think happened, Tom?" Jacob asked.

"I don't know exactly, but I think you're right Jacob, something very bad is happening behind the scenes. It seems like someone is recruiting the elite. I just don't know who or why."

"Maybe we could find this Joshua kid," Kyle suggested.

"I'm afraid I already did," Tom replied, "Joshua's mom worked at the PMC Atlanta Children's Hospital."

"The one on the news?" Jacob asked.

"Yes. The timeline adds up. Apparently, shortly after he escaped, Joshua visited his friends at the hospital. He started on the third floor and healed each kid in every room. He then went to the fourth floor and tried working his way to the fifth floor. My guess is that he sacrificed all his energy making them better. It wasn't on the news reports, but they found his body in the stairwell between the fourth and fifth floors the morning after the healing. I saw his body and his mom's body in the morgue just a few weeks later."

"Do you think Riley is still in danger?" Jacob asked.

"Maybe. If she is, the safest place for her is right here," Tom replied.

"She can stay as long as she needs to. We will keep her safe."

"Thank you so much, Jacob."

"What's the next step for you, Tom?"

"I need to figure out who knows about the elite, who is recruiting them, and why. They may not be just recruiting Class 2."

"What can I do to help?" Kyle asked.

"Nothing right now," Tom replied, "but if someone is recruiting the elite and disabling their chips, there may be a time coming soon for you to fulfill that purpose we were talking about."

Tom turned his attention to Jacob, "I apologize for the short visit, but based on what I just heard, I have a lot of research to do."

"I understand," Jacob replied.

"Will we see you for church tomorrow?" Suzanna asked.

"Yes. Church and lunch, I assume," Tom said with a smile.

"Absolutely," Suzanna said, "I'll expect to see both you and Kyle bright and early in the morning."

"Yes," Tom answered, turning back toward Jacob, "and then, after lunch we can talk about those headaches you've been having."

Jacob gave Robert a glaring stare. Robert immediately pointed at Suzanna who nudged him in the side after his attempt at shedding the blame.

Chapter 28

Tom immediately opened his laptop and logged on to cross reference elite with all reported missing persons. Much to his relief, the list was short. He filtered the list by prioritizing the Class 3 elite. He then searched for the name 'Jeremy'. It didn't take long for his search to find the name 'Jeremy Grimes'.

Jeremy was a high school senior whose body hadn't matured as quickly as other boys his age. Jeremey was so scrawny and fair skinned that most of the time he looked sickly. He had short hair and a face full of acne. Puberty had not been kind to Jeremy, and his classmates often capitalized on his misfortune to make themselves feel better. He was a favorite target of the typical school bullies and couldn't shake his elementary school nickname 'slimy grimy'.

Jeremy attended Northside High School, which was ironically located on the south side of Nashville. The school had more than its fair share of upper-class rich kids as well as the normal high school cliques. Students who didn't fit in with any of the cliques ended up a lot like Jeremy- quiet and reserved on the outside but angry and lonely on the inside. His homelife was as equally dismal. Jeremy's dad and mom divorced when he was little, and his dad didn't really want anything to do with him. Jeremy's mom tried to overcompensate by babying him, but inside, Jeremy grew to resent it.

Jeremy never went looking for enemies, but they seemed to find him nonetheless. His biggest nemesis was Kurt, a star football player who was focused on elevating his status by bringing others down. Kurt's pride and joy was the vintage Camaro that his parents had bought him for his sixteenth birthday. It had been fully restored, and it was the prettiest car in the parking lot. It was deep blue with shiny chrome wheels and air shocks in the back that lifted the tail of the vehicle up like a muscle car.

Kurt always seemed to find new ways of taunting Jeremy to try and make himself look cool. It started with a few immature comments at Jeremy's expense and some pushing around in the hallway, but it soon escalated to much more. The more Jeremy would tolerate and try to avoid Kurt, the more humiliation he would endure.

The height of his disgrace came one day after Physical Education class. Following his normal protocol, Jeremy waited until most of the other guys had showered before he ventured into the locker room shower. It was extremely uncomfortable for him, but it was a school requirement that all students participate in the class, and that every student shower after class. He staged his towel and change of clothes on a nearby bench and quickly scurried into the shower. Not wanting to waste any time, Jeremy lathered and rinsed in just a few seconds and quickly reached out to grab his towel. To his horror, the only article left on the bench was his underwear. He heard the laughter from across the locker room as a group of boys stood pointing and chuckling at him. Kurt waved the pile of clothes in the air.

"Looking for these, Slimy Grimy?"

"Please give those back," Jeremy said in a low voice as he covered himself with the shower curtain.

"What class do you have next, Slimy Grimy?"

"Please, Kurt."

"What class?" Kurt continued to taunt.

"Math."

"Well then," Kurt said with a smile, "I'll leave a trail for you, so you don't forget how to get there. Come on guys, let's make sure Slimy Grimy can find his way to class."

Kurt dropped one sock and then led the group of boys out of the locker room. Jeremy had no choice but to follow them sopping wet and get dressed along the way. The bell had already rung, so there weren't many students left in the hallway. Those who remained were part of the cruel game. Jeremy's face was hot with embarrassment and cell phones throughout the school were flooded with pictures of Jeremy half-dressed and picking up his clothes along the hallway.

A few days after the locker room incident, the bullied became the bully. It began with a stirring in the hallway between classes. Whispers led to students walking out the back door of the school toward the football field in small groups at a time. They came back in just a few minutes after visiting the outdoors, either shocked or laughing under their breath.

Finally, someone was brave enough to tell Kurt what they saw. He bolted out the back door of the school and ran out to the field. He stopped at the edge of the running track that surrounded the field. There, in the middle of the football field, was his prize Camaro. But it was no longer the prettiest car on campus. The windows had been smashed. All four tires were flat, and the body of the car was littered with dents and scratches.

Kurt stood shocked. His faced turned red, and he grit his teeth. Off to his left, hiding behind the bleachers, Jeremy was crouched down watching the whole event unfold and smiling from ear to ear. Seconds later, two teachers appeared on the scene to instruct all the students to go back to class. Kurt wouldn't speak to anyone for the rest of the day. The anger boiled within him as he continued through the school day disengaged. The police came to file a report, but no one had a reasonable explanation for what happened.

When the final class bell rang, Kurt desperately needed an outlet for his anger. He snatched Jeremy from the school hallway and drug him out the back door by his arm. He shoved Jeremy to the ground in the middle of a small patch of woods behind the school.

"Do you know who did that to my car, twerp?"

"Leave me alone, Kurt," Jeremy said as he stood to his feet.

"You do, don't you, Slimy Grimy."

"Stop calling me that."

At that point, Kurt could not contain his rage anymore. He balled his fist and swung at Jeremy, hitting him on the cheek. Jeremy stood his ground and glared at Kurt. He had been on the receiving end of Kurt's scoffing too long. This time, things were different. This time, he wasn't afraid. This time, he wasn't weak.

An hour later, two students came across Kurt's battered body lying unconscious in the woods. He was rushed to the hospital, where he spent a week recovering from bruises, broken ribs, and a fractured jaw. Jeremy had disappeared from the scene. His mom and the police rallied friends and neighbors to form a search party, but Jeremy was nowhere to be found.

Chapter 29

The alarm clock was a rude awakening for Tom, who had stayed up too late researching the missing elite. Riley's story kept replaying in his head as he tried to make sense of it all. Kyle was up at dawn and had coffee brewing in the kitchen.

"Good morning, Kyle."

"Good morning, Tom. The coffee is almost ready."

"You can stay here as long as you like," Tom said with a groggy smile.

"You mentioned going to church this morning?" Kyle asked.

"Yes, church and then Sunday lunch with the Monroe family has become a habit lately. If you don't want to go..."

"Oh, that's not it at all," Kyle interrupted, "I would love to go. Remember, I don't get out much. You said Jacob was having headaches, right?"

"Yes," Tom replied.

"If you don't mind, I'd like to stop at the grocery store to pick up some supplies before we have lunch."

"Sure Kyle. But fair warning—if you are planning on helping Suzanna out with lunch preparations, you should know that she gets territorial about people in her kitchen when she is trying to work."

"Thanks for the tip. I'll keep that in mind."

Kyle had never been to a church service before, but he adapted quickly and followed the cues well enough to fit in. The pastor read a passage from Ephesians chapter five and gave a sermon on the topic of marriage. After the service, Tom kept his word and stopped at the grocery store before lunch. Kyle bypassed the boxed food and spent several minutes in the produce section picking out a variety of vegetables.

"I guess I don't have a lot of what you are used to eating at my place," Tom said as Kyle began loading the grocery cart.

"Well, that is true, but this is not just for us."

"Us? No need to worry about me, Kyle, I'm not accustomed to eating a lot of this stuff so maybe you should just get what you need."

"You do want to be big and strong like me one day, right?" Kyle asked with a smile.

"Very funny. I noticed you were very focused on the sermon this morning," Tom said trying to redirect the conversation, "are you thinking about getting married?"

"No. I've never even been on a date."

"I don't suppose there were a whole lot of ladies to choose from at the farm back home."

"Not at all. Actually, during the message I was thinking about George and Danielle, Walter and Mary, and even the Monroes. I haven't known a lot of people, but the ones I do know have had very good marriages."

"Well, not everyone you know."

Kyle paused with an oversized head of broccoli in his hand. He looked at Tom a bit perplexed.

"You're not married, Tom."

"I was once. It didn't work out."

"I'm sorry to hear that."

"Yeah, me too Kyle, me too."

Kyle finished picking out the fresh produce, and they arrived at Robert and Suzanna's house carrying a few bags stuffed with fruit and vegetables. Suzanna greeted them at the door with a hug and offered to escort Kyle to the kitchen with his grocery bags.

Tom walked into the living room where Christina, Riley, and Robert seemed to be deep in a serious discussion.

"Robert, it's good to see you again," Tom said.

"You too."

"I'm not interrupting anything, am I?"

"Not at all Tom. In fact, you may be just the person to help calm our concerns."

Tom immediately noticed that Jacob was not in the room, but before he could say anything, Christina interjected.

"Jacob is in the bedroom. He got another headache right after church. Tom, I'm really worried about him. The headaches seem to be more frequent each day. Jacob tries to convince me that it's not a big deal and that he can just tough it out, but this never happened before..."

Tom glanced over at Riley.

"She has already offered," Christina said, "multiple times. We let her the first few times the headaches got really bad, but after that Jacob wouldn't let her anymore. He told us he wanted to get to the root cause."

"But he hasn't," Tom interjected.

"No," she replied, "not yet."

Just then, Kyle appeared from the kitchen. "Where is my new super friend?" he asked.

"We were just talking about him," Tom replied, "Jacob is resting in the bedroom. His headaches are getting more frequent and I think we are all wondering if it is related to his restrainer chip. Did you ever experience anything like that Kyle?"

"Let me see if I can help," Kyle said as he disappeared back into the kitchen.

After a few minutes of chopping and blending sounds from the kitchen, Kyle emerged with a cup in his hand.

"What is that?" Christina asked as she stood to her feet.

"Super juice," Kyle said with a smile. "Let's get your man charged back up."

Tom, Robert, and Riley stayed in the living room. They all looked confused as Christina escorted Kyle to the bedroom where Jacob was. He was on the bed with his eyes closed and his hand on his head.

"Jacob," Christina said in a soft whisper.

"Hey, sweetheart," Jacob replied, still keeping his eyes closed.

"Hello to you too, sweetheart," Kyle said with a teasing smile.

"Oh, hey, Kyle."

"I need you to sit up. I have something for you to try."

Jacob partially opened his eyes and sat up on the bed.

"What is that?" he asked.

"Super juice. You're going to love it," Kyle said as he handed Jacob the cup.

"Ugh. It smells terrible."

"Tastes even worse at first, but you'll get used to it. Bottoms up now."

Reluctantly, Jacob took a sip and cringed as the bitter liquid filled his mouth.

"This is nasty," he said.

"Don't drink it like an old lady. Man up. It's best just to chug it all at once."

Jacob hesitated but then took a deep breath and proceeded to empty the remains of the cup. He closed his eyes tight to suppress the gag reflex. He handed the cup to Christina and paused for a few seconds. He opened his eyes and looked at Kyle.

"It's not working," Jacob exclaimed.

"Oh, that's just the first part," Kyle replied. "Now for the fun part. Time to get up. We need to do this next part outside."

Jacob was confused but was willing to try anything to alleviate the pain in his head. Kyle led Jacob outside and stood in front of him. Jacob kept one hand on his head as the pain kept pressing on his skull.

"Push me back," Kyle said.

"What?"

"Push me."

"Kyle, that's silly. I'm not going to…"

"Come on, sissy," Kyle said as he gave Jacob a little shove.

No more prodding was required. Jacob grabbed Kyle by the biceps and pushed as hard as he could. Kyle's feet dug into the ground as he tensed up to provide resistance. Jacob kept pressing harder and could feel his arms throbbing. The two men were locked arm in arm. Kyle took a step back to get a better footing. He gritted his teeth as Jacob increased the pressure. Jacob grunted and shifted his position to engage his back muscles in the battle of wills.

Christina watched from the porch steps still worried about Jacob and unsure of Kyle's tactics. Everyone else watched from the window confused about what was happening. No one said a word as they all witnessed the display of brute force. The strained look on Jacob's face was matched by the look on Kyle's face as they both exerted their energy pushing against each other. The show of strength lasted only a few minutes and left ruts in the grass. With a final grunt, Jacob braced himself and applied all his energy in one final push that sent Kyle to the ground.

Chapter 30

"That's more like it," Kyle said with his signature smile.

"What was all that for?" Jacob asked.

"Tell me how you feel."

"Tired. Warm all over. I can feel my heart racing."

"And your head?"

"It's…it's okay."

"And your stomach?"

"It's hungry," Jacob said with a relieved smile.

"Mine too. Now help me up so we can have some of that famous southern cooking I've heard Tom rave about."

Jacob extended his hand to Kyle, who was still sitting on the ground. The two men walked toward Christina who was sitting on the porch steps.

"Feel better?" she asked.

"Yes. So much better," Jacob replied.

"Good, because you smell worse!"

"Then it's a good thing you married me for better or worse," Jacob said as he opened the door for her. He gently touched her hand as she walked by.

Suzanna and Riley were setting the table as they entered the house and walked to the dining room table. After they all sat down and Robert said a short prayer, Tom questioned Kyle about the exercise.

"How did you know what to do?"

"A lot of trial and error at first," Kyle responded, "Walter and Mary were very insistent that the human body, when fueled right, would manage itself. Even if that body had some supernatural tendencies. I can teach you what I know so you can regulate your strength and take care of your body."

"That would be great, Kyle. Do you think we can do it without the nasty juice?"

"Oh, absolutely not," Kyle said with a smile, "you have to fuel your body with the good stuff God gave us."

"How often will I need to drink that?"

"At least once a week and then you'll need a workout routine that helps burn off some energy too. If you go a few weeks without it, your body will let you know. There are a couple different combinations of fruits and vegetables you can use. I'll show you how to make them."

"I hope the other ones are better than the one I had earlier. It was the worst thing I ever tasted."

"You better show me how to make those," Christina interjected, "just to make sure they are done right, and done often enough."

"I'll help make sure Jake takes his medicine," Riley said in a taunting tone as she looked at Jacob.

"I suspect you will," Kyle said, "I got enough supplies for both of you."

"What?" Riley said surprised.

"Well, I don't know for sure, but I would guess that healing taps the body just like strength. Just to be safe, I wanted to make sure you both had enough to keep you healthy."

Jacob grinned at Riley as her playful countenance disappeared. "Oh, I'll make sure Riles smiles and takes her medicine," he said.

Through the remainder of lunch, Kyle explained more about the diet and exercise routine that Walter and Mary had developed to keep him balanced.

"Certain combinations of fruits and vegetables will last longer than others," he said. "You just need to listen to your body, and eventually you'll actually crave these just like chocolate."

"Now I know you're exaggerating," Jacob replied.

"Kyle, I can't thank you enough for what you did today and your offer to help us," Christina said.

"It's my pleasure. For as long as I can remember, I have wanted to help people. I couldn't really do much of that isolated on the farm. Being here with all of you helps me fulfill that purpose, so I suppose I should thank you too."

"When do you think you will want to go back to the farm?" Christina asked.

"Tom offered to let me stay here for a few weeks, just to help out where I can."

"Well, if you ever need anything, don't hesitate to ask."

"There is one more favor I would like to ask," Kyle said, turning his attention to Tom, "when I met with Danielle, she gave me the contact information for her sister, Wanda. She lives in Alpharetta. I'd like to connect with her and thank her for saving my life."

"I'm sure we can make that happen," Tom replied as they finished their meal and Suzanna began to clear the dishes. Tom then turned his attention to Suzanna as she picked up his plate, "Thank you for lunch."

"You're very welcome," she said, "you guys are welcome anytime."

After lunch, Tom and Kyle left for home. Tom was anxious to get back to his laptop and continue his search for missing elite.

True to his word, Tom arranged for Kyle to meet Wanda later that week. It was an emotional reunion at a local coffee shop just a few blocks from her house. Tom dropped Kyle off to give them some privacy and to run a small errand.

When Tom arrived to pick Kyle up, they were just finishing their conversation. Wanda held a damp handkerchief in her hand as she stood on her tip-toes to give Kyle a hug.

Kyle didn't volunteer much information about their conversation, but he was extremely grateful that he was able to meet the woman who chose life in the midst of a crisis situation.

"Thank you, Tom," he said as he got back in the car.

"You're welcome," Tom replied, "I got you a little something while I was out."

"Christmas was a few weeks ago, and it's not my birthday yet."

"I know," Tom said as he handed Kyle a small bag, "it's not that kind of gift. Open it up."

Kyle reached in the bag and pulled out a cell phone.

"It's linked to my plan, and I already programmed a few numbers in there for you. It's also got a built-in GPS, just in case you ever get lost. I need to do some traveling in the next few weeks and wanted you to have a way to call me or Jacob if you need anything."

"Thanks, Tom. That means a lot," Kyle said as they drove off.

Chapter 31

After Riley's account of her abduction and the introduction of Kyle's super juice, life settled into a routine for Tom, Kyle and the Monroes. Kyle didn't want to go back to the farm until the mystery of the missing elite was resolved. Tom extended the offer for Kyle to stay as long as he wanted. Ten weeks passed with no significant events. Over the course of that time, Kyle made himself at home and got much more familiar with Tom's kitchen. He also took the liberty of hanging a punching bag with some rope and chain on a tree in Tom's backyard close to where his property bordered an undeveloped wooded area. It was out of sight from the neighbors, which gave Kyle the opportunity to work out without risking someone seeing the magnitude of his strength.

In addition to his daily workouts, Kyle also volunteered to paint the new front door and repair Tom's broken furniture from his earlier encounter with Jacob. Tom purchased a gallon of oil-based, dark blue paint for the door but had not taken the time to paint it. Kyle enjoyed painting, and it kept him busy since there seemed to be no action on the horizon. He was meticulous when he painted, taking great care with every stroke. His attention to detail made the door look great, but it took him much longer than

Tom thought it should. Kyle spread the work over several days and made a habit of storing the leftover paint on the rear porch near the back door.

Kyle met with Jacob twice a week at the auto salvage yard in East Griffin to train him on how to regulate his strength and balance his nutritional intake. The salvage yard was isolated from the public and gave the men enough heavy equipment to use for weight training. The side gate was always unlocked, and no one was around after 4:00 each afternoon. Jacob showed Kyle the remains of Christina's wrecked car that changed their lives forever. Retelling the story stirred up a lot of remorse in Jacob. He used that sorrow to fuel his work outs and build his strength.

In return, Jacob taught Kyle how to drive. Kyle was the first to admit that he wasn't particularly good at it. Jacob agreed wholeheartedly. Jacob's truck suffered a few additional dents and scratches. Kyle was very apologetic each time he made a mistake, but Jacob said it gave his truck more character.

As horrible as the super juice tasted, Jacob and Riley both consumed it weekly. Christina thoroughly enjoyed experimenting with different combinations to make the vegetable smoothies, and there were a few combinations that both Jacob and Riley added to a forbidden list. The shared misery of consuming the smoothies helped solidify the relationship between Jacob and Riley. Christina often remarked that they acted like long-lost siblings. Jacob's headaches stopped, and they were finally able to settle into a routine.

Riley got a job at Sam's Pizzeria, the local pizza restaurant in town, where she worked four days a week. Jacob was reluctant to let her at first, but she wanted to feel like she was contributing to the family since they had done so much for her. After much begging and unfair use of the puppy-dog eyes, Jacob relented.

Since Christina was walking again, Jacob invested in a small used car that Christina and Riley shared to run errands. Riley seemed to get more use out of it as a commuter for her new job at Sam's. One day, Riley coerced Kyle into trying to drive the small car, but his large body was so restricted, he couldn't even sit up straight. Christina captured several pictures of the event. It became the basis for several jokes in the weeks that followed.

Tom's search for missing elite resulted in a compiled list of young men and women with no real pattern to link them together. They all disappeared within a three hundred fifty-mile radius of Atlanta, which made Tom suspect that whoever was working behind the scenes was headquartered there.

Tom spent weeks searching through police reports and looking for solid leads only to find a dead end at each turn. He was certain that sinister motives were in play, but whoever was recruiting the elite was keeping a low profile. Tom was able to integrate his search with his existing workload. He sent Bradshaw updates with just enough information to appease him, but without revealing his suspicions that trouble was brewing. Most of his work kept him local, but he did travel to complete some file updates.

The longest trip Tom took was a week somewhere out west. He was extremely vague about the trip during conversation over Sunday lunch, but Kyle noticed that he left with one phone and came back with two—the black work phone that was worn from use and another phone with a blue case that he carried with him but never used.

Chapter 32

The quiet normal routine made Tom anxious. All signs pointed to something ominous on the horizon, but each day felt like status quo. As much as Tom tried to keep the information to himself, Kyle constantly asked him about the missing elite. Reluctantly, Tom shared the little bit of information he had with Kyle.

Riley's kidnapper was Jeremy Grimes, a Class 3 elite from Nashville with super strength. Most of the missing elite were Class 2 healers or Class 3 elite with strength. Included on the list were eighteen-year-old twins Ethan and Ryan Sanders, both Class 3 elite with strength and a history of violent behavior. All of the Class 3 elite on the list were young men in their late teens, while the Class 2 healers were a mixture of girls and boys in their teenage years, making Tom suspect that there was a pattern being followed.

Tom Marshall Personal Log File BJOB1821

I had just over a dozen missing elite on my list. I sorted the list based on risk level. Each of the missing elite had a hardship or trauma in their life that made them susceptible to influence, but I considered some more dangerous than others. Jeremy Grimes was at the top of my list, and there was a personal connection there that drove my desire to track him down. The Sanders boys took the next two slots on my list.

Ethan and Ryan Sanders grew up in Athens, Georgia. Their dad, Billy Sanders, was a high school football star and had high hopes to play college football after graduation. Those dreams were dashed when a car accident injured his knee beyond repair. He drowned his despair in alcohol and started working for his father-in-law selling tires at the local Plaza Tire Mart. Depression and alcohol led to an abusive marital relationship. Mrs. Sanders was a classic enabler who tried to maintain peace in the household. She took most of the abuse to keep him from hitting their sons. She thought she was doing the right thing by protecting them, but the repeated arguments that escalated into physical fights left both the boys with the lesson that violence was acceptable. Ben was their assigned monitor and used to tell me horror stories about their devious and violent behavior. To be honest, the twins were likely more than Ben could handle, but since they were local and he was resistant to travel, there wasn't a better alternative.

On more than a few occasions, the local Department of Family and Children Services was called to visit the family. The boys learned to play the system to get what they wanted and worked well together to advance their cause. According to the records, they ran away from home in early November just a few days after their eighteenth birthday. Their disturbing psychological evaluations and their history made them volatile and dangerous.

Since there had been a history of visits from the Department of Family and Child Services at the Sanders house, I impersonated one of their field auditors to pay a visit to the Sanders. Sheila Sanders welcomed me into their small home and offered me some water. She seemed reluctant to let me in much past the front door. She was an attractive blonde woman in her late thirties, but the shake in her voice and her mannerisms pointed to years of abuse. She acted as though an explosion was imminent at any time.

I could barely see Billy sitting in a recliner in a room toward the back of the house, fully engrossed in a football game on the television. He never even acknowledged my presence the entire time I was there.

Sadly, neither Sheila nor Billy seemed very concerned about the disappearance of their boys. Sheila mentioned that they had run off in the past, but everything always worked itself out. I could tell that she was trying to convince herself more than me.

"They are eighteen years old now, so they need to make their own way. It will all be okay," she said.

"Have you heard from them at all?" I replied.

"No," she said, glancing over at her husband in the back room, "and I don't expect we will. It's probably better that way. It will all be okay."

Every time she spoke, she ended with the phrase, "It will be okay." I wondered how many times she said that phrase in her life, and how long it took to convince herself. I had a great deal of pity for Sheila Sanders. Protecting her sons from physical harm had taken the priority in her life for the past eighteen years, and now she was alone, longing for purpose and love. With some limited knowledge of what I was likely to face at their house, I wrote down the contact information for some abuse help centers in the area on a small business card. After our brief conversation, I handed her the card. I thanked her for her hospitality and left in hopes that she would eventually seek out help.

Tyler Johnson was fourth down on my list, not because I thought he was extremely dangerous, but because he was impressionable. Tyler was the only African American missing elite on my list and based on what Riley told me about her abduction, Tyler was likely spending a lot of time with Jeremy.

Tyler grew up in a public housing development just off Boulevard Street in the heart of Atlanta. His mom died when he was just a baby, so Tyler lived with his father and grandmother. Tyler didn't see his dad very much. When he did, the interaction was usually brief and harsh.

His dad worked several low-income jobs just to pay the bills and was very tough on Tyler growing up. As much as he tried to please his dad, Tyler was never good enough. His dad was never satisfied with the "B+" grade or the point guard position in basketball. Sometimes, he would express his disapproval verbally, but most often he did it with just a disgusted look.

I visited the building where Tyler grew up and met his grandmother. His father was at work. That wasn't surprising. Tyler's grandmother kept me hostage for two hours telling me stories about Tyler growing up. She seemed to fill that motherly need in his life, but her love and concern for him could not fill his need for masculine approval.

"He got on the bus one morning going to school and just didn't come home," she said, "please try to find him and bring him home. I pray for that boy every day."

"Yes ma'am, I will do what I can," I said, finally seizing the opportunity to escape.

There wasn't much hope in her voice as she said goodbye. She had filed a police report but probably thought nobody cared about a missing kid from the bad side of town.

Tyler disappeared around the same time as Jeremy, so I assumed they were teamed up for whatever tasks they were given. One of those tasks appeared to be recruiting other elite.

Below Tyler on the list were a few other Class 3 and Class 2 elites that I considered less dangerous based on their past. Included at the bottom on the list were Riley Bridges, Joshua Goodson, and Alan Brinkley. Alan's body was found in a ditch near downtown Atlanta about the same time that Riley escaped, so I assumed he was the one who planned to escape with Joshua. Obviously, he didn't get away.

Tom Marshall Personal Log File BJOB1821

End of Record

Chapter 33

For the most part, Riley enjoyed her job. She felt more comfortable and safer in the small-town environment of Griffin than she did back home in Charlotte. She worked hard, and it didn't take her long to learn the names of the regular customers and befriend her fellow employees. Sam was the owner of the restaurant and treated her very well. He was in his late fifties and had been managing the restaurant for thirty years. His claim of "the best Italian pizza in Griffin" was unchallenged since his restaurant was the only pizza restaurant in town.

Riley preferred to work dayshift. The restaurant was located next to a daycare center, and she enjoyed hearing the children playing on the playground. To balance shift coverage, Sam asked her to work two nights a week. For safety reasons, Sam always made sure there were two employees each night to close and mandated that they stay together so no one ever left alone. The area of town was relatively safe, but the restaurant was in an isolated location and Sam didn't want to take any chances. Riley didn't mind the work, but the atmosphere of the night shift was a lot quieter and sometimes too eerie for her. Riley had good cause to be concerned.

After helping to close down the restaurant one Friday night, Riley and her friend Brandi locked the doors and walked together to their cars. Riley was typically very conscious of her surroundings, but two figures hidden in the daycare playground equipment in the lot next to the restaurant had escaped her view.

"There's the girl who got away," one of the voices said as they walked briskly together toward the girls. Riley turned quickly toward the voice. She couldn't distinguish the face in the darkness, but she recognized the voice, and it gave her chills down her spine. Riley was speechless. Her friend Brandi was much less intimidated.

"Who are you and what do you want?" Brandi said in a defensive tone.

"I got in a lot of trouble when you ran off. I don't intend for that to happen again."

The tone of the voice was not deep like a man, but still menacing. Riley suppressed her fear and shock long enough to say his name.

"Jeremy."

"You do remember me," he said. As they got closer to the lights of the parking lot, Riley recognized the other boy with Jeremy as the one who was with him when she was first taken. They were now just a few feet in front of Riley and maneuvered themselves between the girls and their cars.

"Who's your friend?" Riley said, directing her stare at Jeremy's eyes.

"This is Tyler. We just want to talk," Jeremy replied.

"Somehow I doubt that," Riley retorted.

"You boys better get out of our way," Brandi said.

"Well, aren't you the tough girl," Jeremy taunted.

Brandi played volleyball on the high school team and was confident in her ability to defend herself if necessary. Unfortunately, she didn't realize just how much she was outmatched. Brandi wasted no time with small talk and tried to surprise the boys with a quick right hook to the jaw of Jeremy's friend. It was an impressive attempt, but Tyler didn't flinch. He responded by grabbing Brandi's arms and turning her around so that he was behind her. His grip on Brandi was painful, and she squirmed to get free. She was now facing Riley, and the panic on her face was evident.

"Stop it, Jeremy," Riley yelled, "let her go or I'll scream."

"You would only be wasting your energy. There's no one around here for miles. Now let's see if you've learned anything since our last encounter."

Jeremy reached behind him and revealed a large military-grade tactical knife. Riley didn't know what to do. She knew he was probably right; if she screamed, no one would hear her. She couldn't run, and she couldn't fight him.

He pointed the knife at Brandi and, with one swift motion, cut her forearm as she was being held tight by Tyler. Brandi screamed as tears welled up in her eyes. She tried even harder to get loose, but the grip was too tight.

Instinctively, Riley moved quickly to her friend and grabbed the bleeding wound. The cut was deep and bleeding heavily. Riley held the wound tight and looked straight into the fear deep within Brandi's eyes.

"It's going to be okay, Brandi. Look at me. Just keep your eyes on me."

Brandi felt the warmth of Riley's touch and began to calm down as the sharp pain subsided. Within just a few seconds, Brandi glanced down at her arm and then back at Riley with a look of amazement.

"Stop it, Jeremy," Riley said in a stern voice, "what do you want?"

"Very nice. You have learned some things since we were together last. You're going to come with us. No fighting and no escaping this time. If we do this the easy way, your friend gets to go home tonight. If not, you will be getting a lot more blood on your hands. I suspect at some point she will run out."

Riley remembered what Joshua had told her about how they kept hurting his mom more and more until the wounds were too great to overcome. Riley was frustrated but didn't see a way out. She lowered her head in despair and said, "Let her go."

Jeremy grabbed Riley by the arm and started walking toward a car in the parking lot next to the restaurant. Tyler shoved Brandi to the ground with a final warning.

"You better not say anything to anyone, or we'll be back and next time, we won't be so nice."

Brandi laid on the ground and watched in horror as they drove off. The shock of the whole incident left her frozen on the parking lot asphalt. She stared at her arm and cried for a long time. After she composed herself, Brandi ran back into the restaurant and locked the door behind her. She immediately called her parents to come pick her up. She was still shaking all over and in no shape to drive. After assuring her they were on the way, Brandi then made a second phone call.

"Hello"

"Mr. Monroe, this is Brandi..."

Chapter 34

Jacob always stayed up waiting for Riley to come home when she worked nightshift. When his phone rang, he assumed that Riley was calling to let them know she would be coming home a bit later than usual. He was so confident it was Riley that he didn't even look at the caller ID. His demeanor quickly changed as he heard Brandi talking through her tears on the other end of the line.

Christina immediately knew something was wrong by the look on Jacob's face, and she rushed to his side so she could hear what Brandi was saying. They both listened to Brandi's account of what happened. They could tell that she was still in shock and more than a little frightened.

"Are your parents coming to pick you up?" Jacob asked.

"Yes sir. They're on their way now. I'm so sorry. I just didn't know what to do."

"Brandi, this isn't your fault. We're going to stay on the phone with you until your parents get there, okay?"

"Yes sir," she replied, still shaken, "I just don't understand. Why did they take her? How did she do that to my arm?"

"Listen carefully, Brandi. What happened tonight wasn't right and we're going to do everything we can to make it right. We're going to find Riley and bring her back, okay?"

"Yes sir," she said with her voice still shaking.

"In the meantime, I need you to promise me that you won't tell anyone else about Riley healing your arm. She has a very special gift and if anyone else finds out about it, she could be in even more danger. Do you understand?"

"Yes sir," she replied as she started to calm down, "my dad just pulled in, so I'm going to go now."

"Ok, Brandi. Thank you for calling us and for being brave. You'll be safe now with your dad. Get some rest, and we'll talk again tomorrow."

"Ok, bye."

Jacob set the phone down for a minute and looked at Christina. His facial expression was a mixture of confusion and helplessness.

"I should have been there. I should have picked her up," he said, staring down toward the floor. Christina put her hand on his chin to pull his focus back to her.

"Jacob, you can't blame yourself for this. We need to figure out how to get her back."

"You're right," he said as he picked the phone back up and dialed.

198

As was his habit, Tom was up late still trying to piece together the events and make sense of it all. After losing his home office room to Kyle, he had set up a spot on the kitchen table to spread out his files. Kyle, in contrast, was already fast asleep. Tom's focus was broken by the sound of his cell phone.

"Hey, Jacob."

"Tom, somebody took Riley."

"What? What do you mean?"

"We just got a call from the girl she works with at the restaurant. They closed up at the end of their shift and as they were heading to their cars, two teenage boys approached them and took Riley."

"Hang tight, I'm on the way."

It was almost midnight when Tom arrived at Jacob's house. Tom thought it best to let Kyle sleep. Both Jacob and Christina were still visibly upset. Jacob relayed everything Brandi had told them about the incident. Tom wanted to jump into action immediately. He felt helpless and desperate. He remembered telling Riley that she would be safe now. That memory produced fear and guilt. He wanted to do something to fix it. They all wanted to do something, but no one knew what to do.

Tom sat back in the chair and talked out his thoughts.

"Why come after her again? Do they need her for something specifically, or are they just covering their tracks since she escaped once already? Surely, they're not afraid of her going to the police. She would have already done that."

"Either way," Jacob interjected, "how did they even know she was here?"

"That is a good question," Tom replied, "have either of you noticed anything unusual in the past few days? Any strangers in the area?"

"Oh my word," Christina said, "Yes. The other day there was a utility bucket truck here working on the streetlight out in front of our house. I didn't recall seeing the light not working, but assumed they were just doing some routine check. I didn't think anything of it at the time."

"Jacob," Tom said, "do you have a tall ladder?"

"I do out in the barn."

"Grab it and a flashlight, and meet me out front," Tom said as he stood to his feet.

The ladder barely reached the top of the light pole.

"What exactly am I looking for?" Jacob asked as he ascended the ladder.

"Anything that looks like it was mounted in the area just recently. Or maybe anything that looks like it doesn't belong," Tom said.

"Got it," Jacob said as he reached up to the top of the light fixture and pulled off a small box that was fastened with two screws. Tom examined the device after Jacob brought it back down.

"What is it?" Jacob asked.

"Self-contained wireless camera," Tom replied, "they've been watching you. That's how they knew Riley was here, and when she would have left for work."

"Is it safe here for Christina?" Jacob asked.

"I think so," Tom replied, "if they wanted a confrontation with you, it would have happened by now. I don't know how much they know about you, but they likely don't want to risk a move on your home turf."

"So, what's the next move?" Jacob asked.

"It's too late at night to do a thorough investigation. I think the only thing we can do is try to get some rest and work on devising a plan in the morning."

Chapter 35

Riley stayed true to her word. She didn't put up a fight or try to escape. She sat quietly in the back seat of the car saying silent prayers in her head. Jeremy had taken her phone and turned it off, so she wasn't sure what time it was, but she felt confident that the drive was less than an hour. She thought it was odd that her abductors didn't blindfold her as they drove to their destination. They traveled down a dirt road to a large compound surrounded by a concrete wall.

Both boys escorted her into an old building and up a flight of stairs to an empty room that only had one small window too high for Riley to see out. The room had a set of shackles firmly attached to the wall with a chain.

Jeremy put her wrists in the shackles and fastened them tight.

"I won't do what you want me to do," Riley said, trying to be brave.

"Don't worry," Jeremy replied with a creepy smile, "we are way past that. We're not going to ask or force you to do anything."

"Then why am I here?" she said as Jeremy and his partner turned to leave the room.

"Relax and enjoy your stay."

As they left, she noticed there was no lock on the door. She pulled the chain tight to see if she could break it loose from the wall, but it held firm. Riley replayed the whole incident in the parking lot over in her head wondering if she should have done something different. She knew Jacob and Christina would be worried about her, and she feared that Jacob might be the one these guys were really after.

If they were using her as bait, she had to get out before her friends fell into a trap. She struggled with the shackles and tried to squeeze her hand through the metal cuff. Her efforts failed. The cuff was just too small, and her hands already felt tender from the attempts. She was completely exhausted. After a few hours of struggling and failing to get free, she fell asleep on the floor.

Riley woke up to find a small jug of water and a plate with bread just within her reach. She ate slowly and examined the bruises on her wrists from the night before. As the hours passed, she became more desperate to escape. She tried to pull the chain from the wall again, but it wouldn't budge. She could tell from the dimming light in the window that it was getting late. If she was going to get away, she was going to have to make a painful sacrifice.

Riley sat down and, with her legs bent, put her feet against the wall. The chain was pulled to its furthest extent and the cuffs were tight against her hands. She made her hands as compact as possible and pushed off the wall with her legs. The pain was excruciating. Tears dripped from her tightly closed eyes and with a final grunt, she pushed as hard as she could off the wall. She heard and felt the cracking of bones in both her hands as they slipped through the cuffs.

She started hyperventilating. The pain was unbearable, and she was afraid to look at her hands. She could feel them shaking uncontrollably. The force of the release left her motionless on the ground. She glanced down at her hands to see the damage. Suddenly, she felt light-headed. A ring of blackness started from the outskirts of her vision and worked its way toward the center of her focus. She rested her head on the cold concrete floor and passed out.

Tom Marshall Monitor Log Personal File BJER487

I got back home late last night and accidently woke Kyle from his sleep. I updated him on Riley's abduction. He felt just as frustrated and helpless as the rest of us. After talking through possible next steps, we both decided to clear our heads by trying to get some sleep. It didn't last long.

My day started at six this morning. I made an honest attempt to get some sleep but failed miserably. From the sounds of the tossing and turning all night in the room across the hall, I assumed that Kyle had similar luck. Several times through the night, I could hear him praying out loud. He wasn't the only one praying. I began to wonder why God would let this happen. I also wondered how much more He would let happen. The questions, prayers, and frustration felt endless. Finally, I decided to get out of bed even though sunrise was still an hour away.

Kyle heard me get up and joined me in the kitchen for an early breakfast. I told him that I planned on being gone most of the day to do some investigation work. He offered to join, but I insisted that he stay at home. I wanted to take every precaution possible to avoid Kyle being exposed as an elite. I felt I owed that much to Walter.

I started by interviewing Brandi. Jacob helped arrange the phone call, and she told me everything that happened. From the shakiness of her voice, it was clear that she was still upset, but if I had waited a few days to talk to her, she may have forgotten some critical details.

My next stop was the pizza restaurant. Sam was very accommodating. He had installed security cameras a few years ago and graciously let me have access to the video files. After meeting with Sam, I was anxious to get back home to compile and analyze the data.

There was no audio on the security footage, but the video gave me some critical information. Most of the confrontation happened just outside the view of the security camera, so I had to rely on Brandi's testimony for the details. The camera did capture the car as it drove away. After zooming in on the back of the car, I noticed it had a government license plate starting with the letter "W". I clearly remembered Brandi describing the knife as an army style weapon. Those two facts led me to suspect the only military individual that knew anything about the elite. The thought turned my stomach. I believed after the incident with Richard that I would never have to cross paths with him again. At this point, it's just a suspicion, but it's more of a lead than I have had for several weeks. I just needed a way to confirm it.

The abduction happened late at night, so I speculated that wherever they took Riley, it wasn't very far. I found two potential locations that seemed to fit the timeline and distance. Fort McPherson was located southwest of Atlanta. It was closed down several years ago and was redeveloped for commercial use. Fort Gillem was located in Forest Park to the southeast of Atlanta and closer to Griffin. Fort Gillem housed several government entities including a crime lab before it closed several years ago. Portions of Fort Gillem were redeveloped as industrial property, but some of it appeared to remain intact and abandoned according to the research.

There is enough evidence to warrant a drive-by without getting too close. If my suspicions are correct, it may be time to pull Bradshaw in for some backup. I just need to confirm some theories first.

Tom Marshall Monitor Log Personal File BJER487

End of Record

Chapter 36

It was late afternoon when Tom decided to further investigate Fort Gillem. Kyle was walking out the door for his typical afternoon workout, while Tom finished his log entry. Tom shut his laptop down, put the computer and George's hard drive in a bag for safe keeping, and headed out the door. He thought he might pass Kyle running on the road as he left, but Kyle was too fast and already out of eyesight as Tom drove away from the house.

Tom parked in a secluded location about half a mile from the dirt road that led to the entrance of the old Fort Gillem compound. The dirt road ran through a wooded area that had not been maintained in years. Still, the area was clearly not totally abandoned. Several sets of recent tire tracks on the road indicated that some amount of regular traffic was happening in and out of the compound. Tom stayed away from the road and walked in the woods in the same direction the road was leading to avoid being spotted.

It wasn't long before Tom encountered a large concrete wall with barbed wire on top of the wall and bare steel wiring attached to the side of the wall at different elevations. He immediately recognized it as an electric fence. The wire and insulators appeared to be in good shape. Whoever was using this fence had maintained it well. It was evident that visitors were not welcome.

Suddenly, Tom heard the rustling of leaves closer to where the road entered the compound. He froze, hoping to remain unnoticed, but the sound kept getting closer. Tom moved away from the wall and squatted near a fallen tree to hide himself as the rustling noise got louder. He could see a young man dressed in camouflage walking along the wall. He looked to be in his mid-teens. Tom tried but couldn't get a good look at his face.

As Tom shifted his weight, a stick under his feet snapped, capturing the attention of the teen who was then just a few feet from where Tom was hiding. The teen glanced over and made eye contact. Tom jumped up and started running through the woods back toward his car. The young man quickly started chasing him. Tom could hear the leaves and broken branches crunch behind him as the young man was gaining ground. Tom feared that his chance of escape was small if his pursuer was an elite.

Tom's fear was realized as the young man caught up to him and tackled him to the ground. Tom tried to pick himself up, but he was instantly knocked back down by the young man's foot. In a desperate attempt to get away, Tom launched himself off the ground to tackle the young man. They both fell to the ground and rolled in the forest debris until he pushed Tom off him and quickly stood to his feet.

"Let me go," Tom said in an attempt to reason with the teen. Tom could feel the pain of the scratches and bruises on his arms and legs. His heart was pounding as he tried to regain enough stamina for another run.

"Can't do that, Tom."

"How do you know my name?" Tom asked, realizing he had been baited into coming to the compound, "who are you?"

"I'm not here to talk. I'm just here to bring you in. Alive, if possible."

"Nobody needs to die," Tom replied, looking at his arms to assess the damage, "in fact, nobody needs to get hurt any more than they already are. We can both just walk away."

"I don't think so," the teenage boy said as he started to approach Tom, "you just got here. And besides, we've been waiting for you."

"Who's we?" Tom asked.

"You'll find out soon enough. Let's go."

"Not happening," Tom said as he took off in a sprint.

After gaining a few yards, Tom was again tackled to the ground. But this time, his attacker was going to ensure compliance. The teen jumped up to grab a low hanging tree branch and broke it from the trunk. He then turned and swung it at Tom's head. Tom fell to the ground and blacked out.

Chapter 37

When Riley regained consciousness, she was unsure of how much time had passed. Her wrists were bruised, and both of her hands were broken. The pain was intense, and her hands shook uncontrollably. It took all of her willpower to cry without making a noise so she wouldn't attract attention. Every minor movement of her hands came with a sharp pain that was almost unbearable. Slowly she pressed her hands together, wincing at every jab of pain. She didn't know if her healing ability would work on her own body, but she had to try. She knew she wouldn't be able to escape with her hands broken. The pain was just too intense. It took all her self-control to hold back the screams of pain. As her hands touched each other, she grasped them together in a praying position, closed her eyes, and sat quietly whimpering. She hoped it would work.

In a building across the dirt road from where Riley was located, Tom woke to find himself tied to a metal chair in a dimly lit room. The walls were dingy, and the floor was bare concrete. His head was pounding, and his body ached. Tom heard a door behind him open and the voice of the young man he encountered in the woods.

"He's up," the voice said.

"Hey," Tom said, trying to get his attention, "what's your name?"

The tactic didn't work. Tom couldn't see the young man, but he was convinced that he had not left the doorway. Even so, there was no response.

"Listen," Tom said trying again, "I know that whoever brought you here probably made you some promises or convinced you this was the right thing to do, but they are wrong. Whatever you're involved in isn't right. I can help you though if you are willing to work with me. We can get you back to a normal life. Whoever brought you here is just using you for your abilities. Whatever they promised, they won't deliver on it.

"Oh, but I already have," said another voice from behind him as a second figure walked through the door. The voice was sarcastic and awfully familiar.

"Tom Marshall," the voice continued as it came closer, "once upon a time, he was the smartest person in the room. He was the master monitor who walked on water. And look at him now."

The footsteps drew closer as he talked, until finally the hidden figure was in view of Tom's peripheral vision.

"Why?" Tom said, trying to suppress the shock.

"I'm just following your guidance, boss."

He continued walking around the chair that held Tom tightly and, as he came out of the shadows, the dim light reflected off his shiny leather shoes.

"Let me remember what you told me on the day the department shut down and I lost my job— 'we need to show some resolve and be willing to do whatever it takes. That is what makes people great.' Are you proud of me now? I'm doing exactly what you told me to do. Whatever it takes. Just recently, I was able to see the performance reviews you wrote for me back then. Phrases like 'overdramatic', 'nervous wreck', and 'incapable of handling stress' really stuck out. I idolized you for years, and all that time you were keeping me down and holding me back from advancement just to make yourself look good. How good are you looking now, Tom?"

"Jeff Rogers."

The memories came flooding back in Tom's head. He recalled Jeff sitting in the office next to his at the department. He remembered how annoyed he would get with Jeff and how much Jeff revered him. Tom never thought he would see any of his old office peers again.

"Well, at least you still remember my name," Jeff said sarcastically.

"I did what I did to help you."

"Help me what, Tom? Help me succeed? Help protect me from being a casualty of the department shutdown? Clearly that didn't work. Or just help me to be more like you?"

"What are you doing, Jeff?"

"I'm making dreams come true. No more dealing with bullies, no more feeling like you aren't special, no more people ignoring you or keeping you restrained."

"This isn't right, Jeff, and you know it. We were both loyal to the department. You signed confidentiality agreements."

"I was, and still am, as loyal to them as they were to me."

"Obviously, that's not true. George would have never allowed any of this."

"Ah yes, George, the most loyal of us all. The man without any secrets. Or maybe he did have a few hidden away. Either way, George isn't here anymore, is he?"

"What did you do, Jeff?"

"Me personally, I didn't do anything. I am just looking for truthful answers and valuable information. I did enough research to know that George had some secret files hidden away. I'm guessing those files contain information that I need to support my cause. I'm also guessing that at some point, he passed that information on to you. After all, you were George's favorite."

"Those are a lot of assumptions, Jeff."

"Assumptions with some solid basis. It seems you know quite a bit about the elite surviving without a functioning restrainer chip."

"So, is that why I'm here then?"

Jeff took the pen out of his shirt pocket and started fidgeting with it, just like he used to do in meetings when the department was still open.

"You're here because you are one of two things—a potential player on our team or a loose end that needs tidying up."

"Our team? Who's your boss? Where is General Corbin?"

"Nice try, Tom. You are a crafty one. Everybody works for somebody, but that is for a later time."

"I'm not interested in playing your game, Jeff. There's still a chance to make this right. There's still time to stop and do the right thing."

"I don't need your lessons anymore, Tom. They weren't that good anyway. And if you're expecting me to divulge everything about our plan, well, I'm afraid you are going to be disappointed."

"They're just kids, Jeff. Just kids who want to have a normal life."

"No, Tom, these kids want to have a better life. They don't want to be picked on anymore, they don't want any more psychological evaluations, they don't want to keep wondering why their father left them or why their mom never shows them affection. They weren't meant to have a normal life; they were meant for a greater life."

"Whose greater life? Theirs or yours?"

"You worked with the department too long, Tom. You bought their lies about keeping the elite safe and protecting society."

"And whose lies are you buying?"

"I can't believe you are still loyal to the mission of the department. Even after they abandoned you."

"I'm loyal to helping and protecting people, Jeff, no matter where the paycheck comes from. So, I'm not going to help you, no matter what."

"You're a hypocrite, Tom. If you really believed that the restrainer chip is helping everybody, then why is Jacob Monroe still walking around without one? You want to accuse me of using these gifted young men and women for my own pursuits, but aren't you doing the same thing?"

"No, Jeff. I did once. It was wrong for me, and it's wrong for you. I have a different life now, a better life. If I wanted to use Jacob, I would have brought him with me, but I came alone. Leave him out of this."

"Don't worry, Tom. You won't be alone very long. Your friend is on his way. We invited him," Jeff said as he walked back to the door and addressed the young man still standing in the doorway, "Cole, go get ready for our special guest to arrive."

218

Chapter 38

Jacob had just arrived home from work when his phone chimed. Both Jacob and Christina were very tired after a short night and very worried about Riley. They committed to stay close to their phones, waiting to hear something from Tom.

As soon as his phone buzzed, both Jacob and Christina ran to the kitchen counter where it sat. Jacob quickly picked up the phone to read the message out loud.

"It's from Tom," he said, *"Jacob, I need your help. I think I found Riley, and she is in danger. Meet me as soon as possible at the old, abandoned Fort Gillem army post in Forest Park. Take the first left once you pass the enclave building but before you get to the industrial park. Keep straight. The street becomes a dirt road and enters a wooded area. Look for the gate at the concrete wall. I'll meet you at the first building on the left. Please hurry."*

Jacob handed the phone to Christina and started putting his work boots on. She reread the message again.

"Something doesn't feel right, Jacob," she said.

"What do you mean?" Jacob replied. He was clearly focused on the mission at hand.

"I don't know. I just have a bad feeling about this. Remember when Tom promised he would never ask you to use your strength again? He gave his word."

"I know, sweetheart, but that was before all this happened. This is Riley we're talking about. I have to help."

"I just don't know."

"Christina, what's the other option? I can't just sit here waiting and doing nothing. I can't ignore Tom's text. She's in danger, and if I can save her and bring her back, then that is what I need to do. Kyle and I have been training, the headaches are gone. I can handle this."

Riley had become like a daughter to both Jacob and Christina. The relationship fueled the passion to do something, anything that could save her and bring her back. Christina still didn't feel right about the situation, but she conceded that the worry of waiting was driving both of them insane.

"Maybe I should go with you," she offered.

"No sweetheart, please stay here. I'll call you as soon as I know something."

"So, you can't just sit here and wait, but I should?"

Jacob paused to collect his thoughts. He stood to his feet and pulled her close. The embrace was silent for a few moments. They had both stopped talking before Jacob broke the silence.

"I love you. I know this is hard, and I'm sorry... But I have to go. The last time I felt like we were in danger, I was safe because of your prayers. That is more important than strength or the power to heal or any other ability. Please, Christina, I need you to pray."

Christina began to cry. She had a lot of bottled-up emotions. To be in his arms and to hear his calm voice gave her a peace inside she had been longing to feel.

"I will," she said, "I promise. I need you to promise too. Promise me that you will be okay."

"I promise," he said as he looked deeply into her eyes one more time, "I'll be back soon."

Jacob followed the directions exactly. Fort Gillem was an old army post originally built in 1941. Several years ago, it was closed and portioned out. The southeast part of the property had become an industrial park. The northwest part of the property remained sealed off and housed an old, abandoned compound. The dirt road led to a complex with a concrete security wall surrounding several buildings. The wall had embedded wiring and looked somewhat dilapidated. It appeared as though there was only one way in or out of the complex. The route had a heavy-duty double gate that attached to the concrete wall on either side. The gate was open wide, and no one seemed to be around. Jacob parked his truck outside the gate alongside the wall and entered on foot.

The sun was sitting low in the sky and was quickly being overtaken by the dark clouds of an incoming storm. Jacob's pace was steady and cautious. He was concerned that he had not intercepted Tom yet, but he was confident in his strength. The adrenaline rushed through his body, making him feel like he could take on any challenge.

Once through the gate, he saw a building to his left and one to his right. The buildings looked identical. Each had a door but no windows on the first floor. The second floor of each building had old windows stained from years of neglect. The door on the building to his left was open just slightly. Jacob remembered Tom's message. As he approached it, he hoped Tom was on the other side. He entered through the door into a room with no other doors or windows. He could barely see a staircase leading to a second floor. It was dark and musty. The only light that came in was from the open door. There were old crates and pallets scattered about. Jacob stopped to listen for footsteps, but he was only met with an eerie silence.

Suddenly, the heavy metal door slammed closed creating an echo throughout the room. It was pitch dark. Jacob could hear movement but couldn't tell who it was or where it was coming from. Before he had time to speak, he felt a piece of wood hit him in the back of the head throwing him off balance. Without time to respond, he was hit again from his left side. He couldn't see his attacker, but he knew from the force of the blow that he was dealing with someone equally matched in strength.

Jacob braced himself, ready to swing in the dark, when another strike came from his right side followed by a hit behind his right knee. Parts of his body began throbbing as Jacob took a swing in the dark but made no contact. He attempted to dodge and weave, but each time he moved, he felt the sting of another blow to his body. His pupils were wide, but there was no light at all in the room. and he couldn't discern where his attacker was.

Jacob took a step back with his arms guarding his head as a wooden board crashed down on him again. He heard the wood crack and break. He heard his attacker break another board off a pallet or crate and the footsteps got closer. Jacob took two more steps back and fell into a hole in the floor. The hole was as deep as Jacob was tall. He felt around to find he was surrounded by rectangular box of cold steel.

He then heard the familiar sound of a hydraulic pump. The cold steel wall in front of him moved toward him. Jacob braced his back against the fixed wall and held his arms out to stop the advancing steel wall from crushing him. His full strength was only slowing the movement as it kept inching closer. Finally, his mystery attacker spoke.

"At full power, that's over one hundred thousand pounds of force," he said. "It's the best industrial compactor on the market and modified especially for people like us. No one is strong enough to stop it. Not even you."

"Who are you? What do you want? Where is Riley?" Jacob grunted.

"Tell me how you get rid of the headaches."

"No," Jacob said as the metal wall continued to advance. His arms were now slightly bent at the elbows. His back was pressed hard against the fixed wall and the ram wall of the compactor was now only inches from his face.

"Suit yourself," the voice said as he walked away.

Jacob could hear him walk up the stairs as the hum of the hydraulic pump filled the dark room.

Chapter 39

As sunset drew near, the clouds above darkened. It was not uncommon to see a rainstorm move in during this time of year. Kyle returned to Tom's house after his run just to keep his body active. He thought it was odd that Tom was not home but didn't really have much reason to be concerned. Schedules and events had become so weird lately. Kyle entered the kitchen area to make a vegetable smoothie when suddenly two young men burst through the recently renovated front door, leaving shards of wood all over the floor.

The two teenagers were as surprised to see Kyle as he was at their sudden appearance. They looked enough alike that Kyle assumed they were the twins. The boys appeared to be in their late teens and clearly were not intimidated by Kyle's size. They approached him together as one of them spoke up.

"Who are you?" one of them asked.

"I'm just the farm-hand," Kyle replied.

"Well, you should have stayed on the farm," the young man replied. He picked up a small end table as he passed it and then threw it down to the floor. The force of the impact splintered the table into several pieces.

"I just finished fixing that," Kyle said.

"The furniture is the last thing you should be worrying about," one of the boys said drawing closer.

"I don't think you want that kind of trouble, boy."

"Trust me, you're the one in trouble. There's two of us and only one of you."

Kyle grinned from ear to ear. "I don't think that will be a problem," he said, maneuvering himself around the counter to confront the boys. He stood firm, waiting for one of them to make a first move. He didn't wait long.

One of the boys tightened his fist and punched Kyle squarely in the stomach. Shocked that Kyle didn't flinch, he redirected his aim toward Kyle's face. Kyle dodged the punch, caught the young man off balance, and pushed him to the ground. The second boy immediately grabbed one of the broken pieces of wood on the floor and swung it at Kyle's head. Kyle grabbed the makeshift weapon before it made contact and jerked it out of the boy's grasp.

"Can't let you mess with the face," Kyle said, taunting the boys, "I don't know what you came here for, but you better leave while you can."

Unwilling to heed the warning, both boys rushed toward Kyle.

Kyle grabbed the countertop with both hands and raised his legs in time for each boy to receive a powerful kick. Both boys flew across the room, with one of them denting the drywall on the other side of the living room. The other boy landed squarely on his back.

"Which one of you is Ethan?" Kyle asked.

"How do you know our names?" one of them said as he pulled himself off the floor.

"I did my homework. You should have done yours, Ethan."

The banter enraged the boys. They simultaneously rushed toward Kyle for another attempt to subdue. him. Kyle braced himself and caught Ethan with a right hook, sending him back a few steps. Just after delivering the punch, Ryan grabbed Kyle from behind and put a choke hold around his thick neck. Kyle stammered backward pushing Ryan into the wall, but his grip didn't loosen.

As Kyle began running out of air. He reached over his head and was barely able to reach the back of Ryan's neck. He gripped Ryan's neck and thrusted forward, sending the teenage boy flying through the air. Ryan's body hit the window that overlooked the back patio, cracking the glass. Kyle charged forward and tackled him, sending both of them through the broken window.

Kyle and Ryan landed on the rear patio with shattered glass all around. As he stood, Kyle grabbed the paint can that was still half full of the blue paint he had used on the front door. In one swift movement, he swung it directly at Ryan's head. It burst open on contact, covering the upper part of Ryan's body, temporarily blinding him as the paint rolled down his face into his eyes.

Just after Kyle launched the paint can, Ethan came exploding through the back door and tackled Kyle to the ground. They rolled for a few feet before Kyle flung him off and sprang to his feet. With Ethan positioned between Kyle and the old oak tree where his punching bag hung, Kyle rushed toward the boy, lifted him off his feet, and thrusted him into the side of the tree. The punching bag fell to the ground. Kyle then shoved Ethan to the ground and held his face into the dirt with his foot. Kyle held him to the ground long enough to tie the end of the punching bag rope to Ethan's left foot. Before Ethan could regain his composure, Kyle quickly threw the rope over a tall branch and hoisted Ethan upside down hanging from the tree.

Ethan swung at the air and squirmed, but there was nothing close for him to grab as he dangled from the tree. A set of car keys, a few loose coins, and a small plastic bag containing two white pills fell from his pocket to the ground. Ryan, somewhat recovered from being blinded by the paint, rushed toward the tree to help his brother, but Kyle had already braced himself and was ready to meet Ryan head on.

Kyle recognized that the strategy that rendered Ethan helpless was the best way to undermine the boys' abilities without permanently harming them. After trading a few punches, Kyle used the chain from the punching bag to hoist Ryan upside down on the opposite side of the tree.

"You're going to pay for this," Ethan said, still struggling against gravity.

"Probably so," Kyle said with a smile, "but not today."

Kyle bent down on the ground next to Ethan to pick up the car keys and the plastic bag with the pills.

"Hey, give those back."

"I'm guessing this isn't your acne medicine," Kyle said, as he put the bag in his pocket.

"I'm going to hunt you down and kill you, man."

"Looks like some rain's coming in. Maybe it'll help cool you off. I'm going to need to borrow this if you don't mind," he said as he held up the car keys.

Both boys continued to try to wiggle their way free as Kyle walked back toward the house.

Chapter 40

Christina's prayer was interrupted by the ring of her phone. She quickly checked the face of the phone before answering it.

"Kyle, are you okay?" she asked.

"I am now. I had a couple of unwelcomed visitors at the house. Tom and Jacob are not answering their phones. Do you know what's going on?"

"We received a text message from Tom. He said that he found Riley and that he needed Jacob's help. Jacob left to go meet him just a few minutes ago."

"Do you know where?"

"Yes, the text said to meet him at the old Fort Gillem army post in Forest Park."

Kyle paused for a moment in an attempt to piece the information together. He could hear the shaking in Christina's voice.

"Christina, are you okay?"

She began to cry. "I'm worried, Kyle. I know I shouldn't be, and I don't want to be, but I'm afraid."

"Things are going to be okay, Christina."

"You're the second person to promise me that tonight," she said. The words helped calm her down, but she wished that she could believe they were true.

"I'm going to go check on them both," Kyle said in a reassuring tone.

"Please be careful. I feel like everyone is rushing into an unknown fight."

"Even you?" Kyle asked.

"Yes," she said, as she paused for a moment. "I'm fighting on my knees. It's what Jacob asked me to do."

"Keep doing that. I'll help you out by giving you one more person to pray for, so you don't run out of words."

The lighthearted comment brought a small smile to Christina's face. "Please call me when you know something, okay?"

"I will," Kyle said as he walked toward what was left of the front door.

Kyle's driving experience was limited to the old tractor on the farm back home and the short lessons Jacob offered. His lack of driving experience, coupled with his struggles to navigate using the map on his phone, resulted in a few wrong turns and more than one dent in the borrowed car. He didn't hit any people or animals along the way, so he considered the adventure a success.

After finally arriving near the compound, Kyle drove up to the main entrance gate that was now closed and securely locked. He immediately noticed Jacob's truck parked alongside the concrete wall, but he didn't see any signs of Jacob or Tom anywhere. He stepped out of the car and walked up to the gate. He could see the small dirt road that led down the middle of the compound with one building on the left and one on the right. There didn't seem to be anyone around. He reached up to touch the gate and felt a powerful shock as electricity surged though his body and jolted him backward. Kyle fell on his back with the sting of voltage slowly dissipating through his body.

After taking a few seconds to recover, he looked around for another way in or around. The concrete walls were tall and thick. The electric fence spanned the wall as far as he could see. Kyle had no desire to repeat that experience.

Kyle got back in the car. He shifted into reverse to create a gap between himself and the gate. He then shifted into drive and pushed the gas pedal all the way to the floor. The car raced toward the gate as Kyle braced for impact. He expected the gate to fly open just like he had seen in a movie, but he was met with disappointment. The front of the car rammed into the gate with a loud crash and then rebounded back a few feet. The airbag deployed hitting Kyle in the face as the car came to a sudden halt.

"Strike two," Kyle said to himself.

White smoke rose from under the hood of the car, and the gate was still intact. The engine of the car had been rendered useless, but it was still a tool in Kyle's eyes. He maneuvered himself behind the car, and with a grunt, he pushed the car as hard as he could into the gate for a second attempt. As the car made contact with the gate, the electricity surged through the body of the vehicle and to Kyle's hands once again, sending him flying backward with an electric jolt.

Kyle lay flat on his back, taking a moment to recover from the electric shock. He looked up at the dark clouds that had been building the sky all evening. He felt a drop of light rain on his forehead. He stared at the sky for only a moment or two and then quietly whispered a prayer.

"God, my friends are in trouble. I believe they are behind this gate, but I can't get through it on my own. Not that I haven't tried. Please, God. You gave me this strength. Please let me use it to help my friends."

Chapter 41

Inside the compound, in a dark, musty room, Jacob Monroe was in the fight of his life. He continued to press against the steel wall, but he was losing ground with every passing second. The thick metal plate was just an inch away from his face, and he felt as though his body was drained of all power. He had never been claustrophobic, but the continuous shrinking of space stirred up a panic and anxiety he had never felt before.

His emotional state was also tapped. He felt guilty for his overconfidence in his strength. And he remembered his final words to Christina. He had promised her that he would be okay. He had given her his word that he would be back. He was faced with the very real possibility of breaking that promise. The more he thought, the more his heart broke.

"Oh God," Jacob said in desperation, "I am so sorry. I relied on my strength, and it can't save me. Please help me. Please…for Christina. I love her so much."

The cold steel wall pressed against his face and was still moving closer. Time had run out, and his strength had run out. He pictured Christina kneeling at the foot of their bed praying, just as he had seen her do many times before. He could imagine in his head her passionate prayer as she begged God for mercy and grace.

Christina was, just as Jacob had imagined, kneeling at the foot of their bed. Her prayer wasn't wordy or complicated. She didn't know what to say, so she just kept repeating what was on her heart.

"Please God, please save my family. Please God. Please save my family..."

She repeated those phrases over and over. Jacob turned his head, and he could feel the pressure of the wall against his cheek and hard pressed against his chest. He had nothing left. He closed his eyes, took one final breath, and echoed Christina's prayer.

"Please God."

Suddenly, a flash of lighting appeared just outside the compound, followed immediately by a massive crack of rolling thunder, and then silence. The hum of the hydraulic pump stopped. The entire compound was shrouded in darkness. Within a few seconds, the emergency power lights flickered on throughout the compound, including a small light on the wall in the room where Jacob was trapped. The pressure stopped, but he couldn't force the hydraulic ram back. He was stuck with only enough room to breathe.

Outside the compound, the flash of lightning almost made Kyle jump out of his skin. It felt and sounded so close. He listened for the faint hum of the electric fence but heard nothing. The power outage gave him the opportunity he was looking for to break through the gates and find his friends. He took two steps back and charged the gate with the full force of his strength. The gates swung open just as the emergency lights came on. Kyle quickly noticed two buildings, one to his left and one to his right. He turned toward the one on the right and kept running full speed.

Being trapped in such a tight spot only allowed Jacob to take small breaths, but he was grateful for each one. He heard the sound of the gates as they flung open outside and then silence once more. The silence was broken by the sound of light footsteps coming down the stairs. He knew that whoever was coming would likely start the compactor. The metal walls were so tight against his head that he couldn't turn to see who it was. He kept motionless and tried his best to quiet his desperate breathing.

Suddenly, he felt a hand on the top of his shoulder. Warmth radiated from his shoulder down to his body, and he could feel his muscles tighten once more.

"Jake," she said, "it's me."

Tears of relief swelled in Jacob's eyes.

"Riley. Thank God."

Adrenaline rushed through Jacob's body as his strength was being restored through her touch. Jacob took a deep breath and pushed against the steel wall that was pressed up against him.

The metal creaked and popped. Then the steel wall shifted. Jacob pushed harder, and the sound of bolts breaking within the giant machine echoed through the room. Jacob grunted and pushed even more as the steel gave way. Within a few moments, there was enough room for him to climb out of the compactor. Jacob rose and hugged Riley tightly.

The reunion was short lived as more footsteps were coming down the stairs. Two men came running down the stairs, each with a handgun. As soon as they reached the bottom of the stairs, they began firing their weapons. Jacob spun Riley around to shield her with his back. Both men fully discharged their weapons and paused to reload. Jacob turned around and recognized one of them as the man who had held the gas mask on Richard's face until there was no more life left in him.

Jacob reached down to grab an old pallet that rested on the ground. He flung the pallet toward the two men, who dodged the projectile. He then grabbed Riley's hand and ran for the door. Jacob surged through the door, flinging it off the hinges with Riley following close behind.

They both noticed some commotion happening in the building directly across from them, but they didn't take the time to stop and investigate. Jacob picked Riley up in his arms and ran as fast as he could toward the broken gate. As they neared the gate, Riley looked behind them to see the body of a young man fly out the window of the building across the road.

Chapter 42

Kyle ran full speed into the door of the building, breaking the lock. Much like the building across the dirt road where Jacob was, the ground floor of this building appeared to be a secure storage area. He was met with immediate gunfire as two men dressed in camouflage opened fire. Kyle ducked behind a large crate as the bullets flew around him. He shoved the crate toward them, and they jumped out of the way to avoid being hit.

Before they could react, Kyle was upon them and relieved both of them of their weapons. He then quickly went up the stairs to the second floor. The top of the stairs led to a long hallway with rooms on both sides. All the rooms to his left had exterior windows that faced the road splitting the compound. The rooms on the right only had one door to enter or exit. He paused to listen for the sound of movement. After a few seconds of silence, he cautiously started walking down the hall, looking in each room.

As he glanced in one of the rooms, out of the corner of his eye, Kyle saw a young man barreling toward him. Kyle dodged just in time to avoid a full body tackle, sending the young man to the ground. He rolled over to get up but was stopped by Kyle's firm grip on the back of his pants. Kyle picked him up by his belt loops and threw him toward the window. The window shattered as he flew through it and plummeted to the ground below. As Kyle watched the young man hit the ground, he saw Jacob carrying Riley, running toward the gate.

Kyle picked up the pace of his search and finally found the room where Tom was still tied to the chair.

"Tom, are you okay?" Kyle blurted, rushing to his side.

"Yes. How did you find me? Where's Jacob? Have you seen him? Did you find Riley?"

"That's a lot of questions," Kyle said, ripping the last piece of rope that held Tom to the chair. "Jacob is okay. I saw him just a minute ago running for the gate. He got Riley. They're okay."

Kyle didn't have time to answer any more questions as a man with leather shoes suddenly appeared in the doorway, accompanied by two men dressed in military fatigues.

"Who are you?" the man asked.

"A friend," Kyle responded.

"A friend?" the man questioned.

"His." Kyle said pointing at Tom. "Not yours. Who are you?"

"Not the guy you want to mess with," he said, turning his attention to his two escorts, "kill them both."

Both men drew their handguns and opened fire. Kyle shielded Tom from the bullets until both men had fully discharged their weapons.

"Impressive," Jeff said, "looks like we aren't that different after all, Tom."

Suddenly one of the men threw a canister in the room and closed the door. The canister rolled to the center of the room and started producing a thick yellow smoke. Kyle quickly removed his belt and looped it around the belt loop at the back of his pants.

"Hold your breath and close your eyes. Grab the end of this belt and get ready to run," Kyle said.

"Where are we going?" Tom asked as he grasped the end of Kyle's belt.

"Through the door, across the hall, through the wall, and out the window. Hold on tight. Here we go."

Tom was certain he could have come up with a better plan, but there wasn't time to argue as the yellow smoke filled the room. Kyle started running toward the door with Tom following about two feet behind, holding his breath the whole time. Kyle destroyed the door and kept moving in a straight line toward the wall on the opposite side of the hall. He smashed though the wall, creating a hole big enough for Tom to follow and kept moving to the window. Just before hitting the window, Kyle turned around and pulled Tom to his chest as he flew backward through the window. He hit the ground with Tom landing on top of him.

Tom grunted as he landed. "I think I broke a rib."

"I know someone who can help with that," Kyle said, standing to his feet.

"Not everyone is as tough as you," Tom said, pulling himself off the ground at a much slower pace than Kyle.

"I did tell you to eat your vegetables," Kyle joked.

"Not now, Kyle. Let's get out of here."

Both Tom and Kyle quickly started running for the gate. Several men came out of both buildings and started chasing after them. As soon as they passed the front gate, Tom stopped and looked around.

"Where's the car?" he said.

"It's over there," Kyle said pointing to the wreckage. "I don't have much driving experience."

"Obviously. We can't get away in that."

They both looked down the road to see a familiar pickup truck coming around the corner. Jacob's truck pulled right up to Tom and Kyle, and they both immediately jumped in the truck bed. The truck kicked up dirt as Jacob hit the accelerator.

A green jeep followed in pursuit as the truck sped down the dirt road. Kyle looked around for anything in the bed of the truck that he could use as a projectile. He found an old wrench. He grabbed it, stabilized himself, and threw it at the jeep. The wrench hit the front grill of the jeep, penetrating the radiator and sending a puff of steam into the air. The direct hit stopped the pursuers as water gushed from underneath their vehicle.

"Thanks for the ride," Tom shouted to Jacob, "how did you know?"

"You can thank Christina for that," Jacob shouted back. "We called her as soon as we got in the truck. She said Kyle was at the compound, so we turned around."

"She's a keeper," Tom yelled.

"Yes, I know," Jacob shouted, "what do we do now?"

"That's a good question. I wish I had a good answer."

Chapter 43

"Pull over, Jacob," Tom shouted from the bed of the truck.

Jacob pulled off the road near an old, abandoned building Tom was pointing to.

"Why are we stopping?" Jacob asked.

"I left my car here. I didn't want to raise suspicions by parking right next to the gate," Tom said as he stepped down from the bed of the truck, holding his ribs.

"Yeah, I guess that wasn't the smartest move," Jacob said to himself.

"Are you okay?" Riley asked as she watched Tom get out of the truck.

"Tom jumped out of a window and hurt himself," Kyle answered with a smirk.

"It would have been easier if you were softer," Tom said, wincing in pain.

Riley rushed over to Tom. "May I?" she said.

"Please," Tom responded. Riley gently slipped her hand up Tom's shirt and pressed softly against his chest. The pain subsided, and Tom took a deep breath. "Thank you, Riley."

"What now?" Jacob asked after giving Tom a second to recover.

"I need you to call Christina and your parents. Tell them to pack up any valuables and some clothes. They may not be safe at home. Kyle and I will go back to my place to do the same."

"About your place, Tom," Kyle interjected, "it may not look the same as when you left it."

"What do you mean?"

"Probably some things I need to explain to you on the way," Kyle said, intentionally being vague.

"Ok," Tom said, trying to get back on track, "please grab only what you need."

"Where are we going?" Jacob asked.

"I'll text you as soon as I know. Please be careful, and let's move as fast as we can."

"Wait," Jacob said, "how will we know it's you? The last text I got from you didn't turn out so great."

"Good point," Tom replied, "I'll end my text with the letters 'DON' in honor of George. Now, let's go. I want to get all of you in a safe place as soon as possible."

Kyle explained his confrontation with the twins on the way back to Tom's house and apologized for the damage. Both Tom and Kyle expected to see the twins still hanging from the tree where Kyle left them, but they were gone.

"Sorry," Kyle said, "I thought that would hold them for a bit longer. I guess they wiggled free. I just wanted to subdue them without hurting them too bad."

"It's not your fault, Kyle. You did the best you could. I was hoping not to drag you into this..."

"But I'm all in now," Kyle said with a smirk. "It's okay, Tom. I chose this, and to be honest, it felt good to use my gift for something more than plowing a field."

"Thank you again, Kyle. I owe you."

Tom and Kyle quickly packed some clothes and essentials in their own suitcases. Tom stepped out on the back porch to make a phone call. It seemed like he wanted some privacy, so Kyle didn't probe him about it. He did make a mental note that this was the first time Tom used the phone with the blue case.

Kyle was waiting in the living room when Tom entered through the remains of the back door. Tom stopped to notice that Kyle had his suitcase in one hand and a large bag in the other with the blender sticking out of the top of the bag.

"You're taking the blender?"

"And the veggies too," Kyle said, "you really are missing out."

"I've seen the face Jacob makes when he drinks those," Tom responded, "I think I'll pass."

Jacob called Christina on the way home to assure her that everyone was okay and to give her the instructions that Tom had provided. True to her character, Christina grabbed the photo albums first and then packed bags for herself, Jacob, and Riley. Jacob called Robert and Suzanna to update them as well and told them to pack up any valuables and standby for instructions.

As Jacob's truck pulled up to their small house, Christina ran out in the wet grass and wrapped her arms around Jacob.

"I was so scared, Jacob," she said with tears lining her face. Jacob buried his chin in her neck.

"I was too, sweetheart. But it's all going to be okay now."

Riley walked around the front of the truck from the passenger side and stood close to Jacob and Christina as they continued their embrace. As soon as Riley got close enough, Christina reached out and pulled her into the group hug.

"I'm so glad you're back, Riley," Christina said, still holding her close. "We were so worried about you. Are you okay? Did they hurt you?"

"No, I'm fine," she said, enjoying the embrace. "I think I was just the bait. They wanted Tom or Jacob."

"Do we know why?" Christina asked.

"Not yet," Jacob replied, "but we're meeting back up with Tom, so maybe we can get some answers. Did you pack up everything we need?"

"Yes. It's all ready to go."

"Great. Let's load up the truck. Tom said not to waste any time."

Just as he was talking, Jacob's phone buzzed. He looked at his phone to see that he was on a group text message with Robert and Tom. The message originated from Tom and only showed the address to an apartment complex in downtown Atlanta. The text ended with 'DON'.

"That's our cue," Jacob said.

"Do you recognize the address?" Christina asked.

"No, but Tom said it would be safe."

Chapter 44

Robert and Suzanna were the last to arrive at the apartment complex. Suzanna ran up to Jacob to give him a hug.

"Are you okay, son?"

"Yes, Mom. I got bruised up, but I'm fine. We're all fine."

"Sorry it took so long," Robert interjected, "your mom couldn't figure out how to get the entire house packed in the trunk of the car."

Suzanna gave him a disapproving look and was about to respond to his comment when Tom interrupted.

"I can imagine this has been very stressful for all of you," he said, "and I'm sorry. This whole situation has escalated beyond my control, and all I can do now is try to keep everyone safe while I figure out the next move. I know this is inconvenient and uncomfortable, but right now, this is the best thing we can do. Thank you for understanding."

Tom's calm tone gave everyone the chance to take a breath and try to recover from the shock of the evening. He continued.

"We have three rooms reserved here for the night," he said as he handed a set of keys to Robert and another set to Jacob,

"It's pretty late, and we've all been through a rough night. We're safe here for now, so let's all get some sleep."

Everyone agreed with Tom's recommendation.

"If you don't mind," Robert said, "before we split up, I know you all have been through a lot this evening, so I'd like to pray for us."

Tom nodded in agreement as Robert grabbed Jacob's hand and then reached for Suzanna's hand. Tom was a bit uncomfortable at first, but then quickly joined the prayer circle as Robert closed his eyes and began to speak.

"Father, I want to thank you for keeping my loved ones safe tonight and for being our peace in times of trouble. I pray that you will guide us to know the next steps to take. I pray too that truth will be revealed, and that the people who are spreading deception for their own personal gain will be held accountable. Please give our bodies rest tonight as we wait to see you work. Amen."

"Amen," the group echoed.

The rooms were each self-contained apartment suites with a small kitchen, living area, and two bedrooms. The beds were somewhat uncomfortable, but after the drama of the past few days, no one complained.

Staying true to his routine, Kyle was the first one awake. He made use of the small coffee machine to hold him over until Tom woke up. The rescue had left him a bit drained. He knew that he needed a vegetable smoothie, but the supplies were still in Tom's car. He didn't want to wake Tom up to get the keys that were in his room. As Kyle waited, he sat on the couch, reached for the television remote, and turned on the local news.

Breaking news from the Atlanta area today. Last night, two teenage boys were found fleeing from what they described as a secret organization recruiting special young men and women...

Kyle jumped up and ran over to Tom's bedroom door. He knocked frantically.

"Tom, get up. You need to see this," he said, "hurry."

Tom jumped out of bed and followed Kyle into the living area as the news story continued.

The story gets even more bizarre. When the boys were found, they claimed they had superhuman abilities. Authorities initially dismissed the claims, but after medical testing late into the night, their claims were found to be true. The boys also claimed to have been recruited by a former government official to be trained for special missions. More on this developing story after this word from our sponsors...

"This is just the break we need," Tom said running back into his room to throw on some clothes. "This is what Robert prayed for. Here is our answer. You must have knocked some sense into them. With the testimony of these boys and my evidence, we can expose Jeff's operation and get the support we need to shut it down. The timing is perfect. I couldn't have planned it better myself."

Suddenly Tom's phone rang, and he reached over to the nightstand to take the call while Kyle muted the television.

"Tom, Bradshaw here."

"Yes sir. Good morning."

"We need to talk."

"Yes sir. I completely agree."

"Where are you right now?"

"Um...downtown."

"Are you near the office building?"

"Not very far. I can be there in just a few minutes."

"Get here as fast as you can. Time is of the essence."

"Yes sir. On my way."

Tom hung up the phone and continued rambling as the future scenario played out in his head. He didn't give Kyle any time to interject as he finished dressing and started for the door.

"Stay here, Kyle. Please check on the others when they get up and wait for me to return."

Tom sprinted out the door without another word. Just a few minutes later, Kyle heard someone frantically knocking at the door. He opened the door to see Jacob with a panicked look on his face.

"Are you okay, Jacob?" he asked.

"Where's Tom?"

"He got a call from Bradshaw to come to the office, and he ran out the door. He saw the twin boys on the news. It looked like they were confessing everything. He said that it was just the break we needed."

"So, wait, you saw the whole news story?" Jacob asked.

"Well, the first part of it. Tom was so excited. He threw on some clothes and left right away. He didn't even take his computer or hard drive."

"Neither of you saw all of it?"

"No. We got interrupted by the phone call. You're freaking me out a bit Jacob. What's going on?"

"Get your boots on and juice up. We need to go."

"All my supplies are in Tom's car."

"I'll have Christina make you one to go. Meet me downstairs at my truck in five minutes."

Chapter 45

Tom envisioned a dozen scenarios in his head on the short drive to meet Bradshaw. It was odd for the downtown traffic to be so heavy for a Sunday morning, which was testing Tom's patience. He probably could have walked faster than the drive. He was very anxious to update Bradshaw on his theories, information, and his experience at Fort Gillem. When he arrived at the building, he noticed two armed gentlemen standing at the door and quite a bit of activity surrounding the building.

Tom kept his brisk pace as he entered the building and walked up a set of stairs to the conference room, where he first met Bradshaw. There were several people in the building, but no one Tom recognized. He assumed they had repurposed the facility for another agency of some kind.

Tom approached the conference room and saw Bradshaw through the glass. He was sitting at the conference room table watching Tom walk toward him. His face was expressionless. Tom entered the room quickly.

"Good morning, Mr. Bradshaw. We have a lot to discuss."

"Yes, we do. I'm going to cut straight to the point with you, Tom. What's going on, and how are you involved?"

"I have discovered a small organization that is recruiting the elite, disabling their restrainer chips, and training them for something. I don't have a lot of details, but I do know where they have been hiding out. If we move quickly, we can shut this down before anything really bad happens."

"Are you wanting some type of plea bargain?" Bradshaw asked.

"Excuse me?" Tom replied, "plea bargain for what?"

"Last night two boys were found fleeing from an area right around your neighborhood."

"Yes sir, they are Ethan and Ryan Sanders, twins and Class 3 elite who were recruited..."

"By you," Bradshaw interrupted.

"What? No, that's not true at all."

"That is what they are claiming. They said that you were building an army of super soldiers, and that you tricked them into joining your organization."

"No sir. That is a lie."

"They also said that you kidnapped a teenage girl, Riley Nicole Bridges, from her hometown, and she is now in your custody."

"No. I mean, she is in my care now, but I didn't kidnap her."

"Did you have permission from her parents or guardian?"

"No sir. Her parents are dead, and her grandmother was her guardian, but she was killed."

"So, she, as a minor, is a ward of the state. Did you take a ward of the state across state lines?"

"Yes, but she was in danger and…"

"The boys claimed that someone named Jacob Monroe, also an elite with a disabled restrainer chip, is working with you as an accomplice. Is that true?"

"Jacob and I are friends, but we're not working together. They're not telling you the truth."

"Is he an elite with a disabled chip?"

"Yes, but George knew about that and he was planning on getting that taken care of."

"George Miller is gone, so the responsibility to do the right thing falls on you. Have you scheduled him to get a new chip?"

"No sir."

"It's been several weeks since George died. You had plenty of time to make that right, but you didn't. Listen, Tom, you're here because of the benefit of the doubt. I like to hear both sides of the story before condemning someone. These boys are making some serious accusations. It appears that there has been a significant increase in the number of disabled or malfunctioning restrainer chips and, right now, everything points back to you."

"I assure you, Mr. Bradshaw…"

Although Bradshaw said he wanted to hear Tom's side of the story, he didn't let Tom finish his sentence before he continued his interrogation.

"The first case of an elite on the loose was Richard Hall. He was one of your former assignments, correct?" Bradshaw asked as he looked down to read the file folder in front of him.

"Yes sir."

"And then Jacob Monroe, also one of your clients, correct?"

"Yes sir."

"And, as a former monitor, you were one of the most knowledgeable in the business. Is that correct?"

"Also true."

"And now we have two young men with a pretty incriminating story who seem to know a substantial amount about the elite and the monitoring department."

"I swear, Mr. Bradshaw, what they're saying isn't true. I've been trying to stop this ever since I suspected someone was recruiting the elite and disabling restrainer chips."

"Which has been how long exactly?"

"Several weeks now and..."

"And you didn't think it was prudent to update me?" Bradshaw asked as he became visibly irritated.

"I was waiting to get enough evidence..."

"You're in a lot of trouble here, Tom. At a minimum, you failed to keep the elite out of the public eye, something you committed to me you would do, and you kidnapped a minor from the state of North Carolina. At a minimum, you withheld critical information from me and jeopardized my reputation as the leader of this effort to regain control of the former monitoring department. In your position, these acts can be considered sedition and maybe even treason. I trusted you because George recommended you, but I am seriously questioning that decision."

"Sir, I can explain."

"Tom, you are under arrest until we can get this sorted out," Bradshaw said with a straight look on his face. He motioned for two men standing in the hallway to enter.

"Mr. Bradshaw, if you give me a chance…"

"I think it's probably best to wait until you get a lawyer before you say anything more, Tom."

Tom sat silently. He was completely unprepared for this situation, and the shock left him speechless.

The two men each took one of Tom's arms, lifted him up from the chair, and placed handcuffs on his wrists in front of him. Bradshaw looked at the one closest to him to give him some direction.

"Take him to the holding facility on Buckeye Road."

"Yes sir," the gentleman replied as they escorted Tom out of the building and into the back seat of a black sedan.

Chapter 46

Tom was in complete shock. The meeting with Bradshaw changed Tom's position from hero to villain in just a few short minutes. He thought for certain that the revelation of Ethan and Ryan as elite was God answering their prayer. He sat in the back of the government car with his hands still handcuffed in front of him and his mind at a loss. He could imagine how Richard felt the day he was arrested. He was shocked, humiliated and on his way to jail.

Both of Tom's escorts sat silently in the front seat. The stop and go traffic of downtown Atlanta was almost a predictable rhythm as they traveled one block at a time, stopping for traffic lights and pedestrians.

After the third consecutive traffic light, the car stopped and waited for a small group of pedestrians to cross the street. A man paused directly in front of the car. A familiar pickup truck pulled alongside the car, and Tom looked over to see Christina in the driver's seat of Jacob's truck. He looked ahead to see that the man standing in front of the car was Jacob. Suddenly, the rear of the car raised in the air, causing the back wheels to lose contact with the road.

In a panic, the driver pushed the accelerator to the floor, but the car didn't move. Jacob came around to the side of the car and pulled the door open, breaking the lock. He then grabbed Tom's arm and quickly pulled him out.

"Get in the truck," Jacob said.

Tom glanced back to see Kyle holding up the back of the car, keeping it completely immobilized. Tom quickly hopped in the passenger side of the truck. Kyle dropped the car a little too hard, breaking the rear axle and jolting the two government escorts inside. Jacob and Kyle both jumped in the back of the truck as Christina pulled away, leaving the two agents stranded.

When they arrived back at the apartment complex, Kyle removed Tom's handcuffs and they all met in Tom's room to talk.

"How did you know?" Tom asked Jacob.

"You missed the best part of the news story," Jacob replied. "Those boys called you out by name and said you were building a superhuman team of gifted individuals. Once Kyle said you left to meet with Bradshaw, we figured you were walking into another trap. We waited outside the office building until we saw those guys escort you out."

"Walking into a trap is happening too often for my comfort. Thank you for coming to get me...all of you."

"Saving your life is becoming a habit," Kyle said with a smile.

"I honestly don't know where to go from here," Tom said.

"Let's start with what we already know," Robert suggested.

"Good idea," Tom responded, "I suppose since we're all on the run now, I owe you some explanations. We know that Jeff Rogers, a former monitor like me, is involved in an effort to recruit and train some of the elite. He is probably the one who set up the remote server access, so we can assume he has access to all the data on the elite, except for the information on George's hard drive. I suspect General Corbin is also involved, but I don't have any proof of that just yet."

"I saw one of the General's men at the compound," Jacob interjected. "It was the same guy who was there when they took Richard down."

"That's confirmation enough for me that the General is involved, and it makes sense that he has something to gain by training a team of elite as a military advantage. What else did you see at the compound?"

"The inside of a trash compactor. Not much more. They had a trap set for me, and I walked right into it. When I arrived, they caught me off guard by closing me in a pitch-dark room where this one guy beat on me pretty hard. He had to be a Class 3 elite."

"That's odd," Tom said, "I heard Jeff tell this one kid to get ready for you to arrive, but he called him 'Cole'. There isn't a Class 3 elite on my list by that name. Did he say anything to you?"

"Whoever he was, he had a mean swing, and he didn't have any problem seeing in pitch-black darkness. When I asked him what he wanted, he asked me how I got rid of the headaches."

"They know how to disable the chips," Tom said, "but they don't know how to deal with the headaches. That may be what they were looking for at George's house. His secret weapon was more than muscle, it was information."

"And," Kyle said, "maybe what they were looking for at your house too." Kyle reached in his pocket and pulled out a small plastic bag with two small white pills in it. "When the twins came to your place, this fell out of one of their pockets."

"Let me take a look," Christina said, reaching for the small bag, "It looks like a type of Fentanyl. It's a heavy-duty painkiller. We used to process these at the medical lab and had to keep them secure so they didn't get out on the street. I can send these to Holly. She still works at the lab and can verify for me."

"If you're right," Tom said, "that must be what they are using to deal with the migraines."

"It's cheaper and easier to make than a lot of other street drugs," Christina responded, "and highly addictive."

"Do you have any idea what they are being trained for?" Jacob asked.

"No," Tom responded, "but they have had plenty of time. According to my records, some of these kids went missing early November last year, shortly after the incident at Camp Pennington."

"What's our next move?" Jacob asked.

"If I may interject," Robert said.

"Please," Tom responded.

"We've all done a lot of reacting lately and rushed into some pretty dangerous traps along the way. If we're safe here for a few days, I think we need to lay low, pray, and wait for the next step to become apparent."

"That is a good suggestion," Tom said, "We have these apartments reserved for a couple of days under someone else's name, so I think we are pretty safe here. If we stay underground and quiet for a few days, it will be harder for anyone to track us down. Everyone needs to shut down their cell phones so we can't be tracked. I have enough cash to keep us alive with groceries for a few days. I, for one, could use a couple days of quiet."

Chapter 47

Kyle found himself back in a kitchen he was unfamiliar with and as usual, was the first one awake. Tom woke to the sound of clamoring as Kyle performed his morning routine of making coffee. Tom came out of his bedroom and joined Kyle on the couch as the morning news came on the television.

"Good Monday morning, Atlanta, and what a weekend it has been! I'm your host Alyssa Bush."

"Heroes among us. This story has captured the attention of the entire nation. Today we have a follow-up story on the two eighteen-year-old boys who were found this past weekend to have superhuman strength. We have an exclusive live interview with Ethan and Ryan Sanders, conducted by our own Shelley Bailey in the parking lot of the news studio. Shelley."

"Good morning, Alyssa. Here with me this morning are Ethan and Ryan Sanders. Good morning to you both."

"Good morning, Shelley," Ethan replied.

"You two have become quite the instant celebrities. Please, share your story with us if you don't mind."

Both boys were seated in director style chairs across from Shelley to the right of the camera. Ethan was more extroverted than his brother and did most of the talking.

"Well, my brother and I are just two normal guys. We both played on our high school football team and did things every normal teenager does. Then, one day, this guy comes up to us and asks us if we want a job. We didn't know who he was, so initially we refused. Then he said we could try it out for just a few hours, and he would give each of us one hundred dollars. When we asked what the job was, he said that it was to test a new virtual reality game. We had seen something like that on television and it looked pretty cool. We also needed the money to help our mom get the medicine she needs, so we agreed and went with him."

"He took us to this place that looked like a science lab and had us sit in these chairs. He put the virtual reality glasses on our heads and a controller in our hands. The game started, and it seemed harmless. All of the sudden, we both felt someone holding us down in the chair and a sharp pain in the arm like someone was giving us a shot. It hurt so bad, but we couldn't get up."

"That sounds terrible," Shelley said. "Did they do anything else to hurt you?"

"No, that was the worst. The man said he was sorry that he had to trick us, but it was because we probably wouldn't have believed him and let him give us the shot otherwise. After that, he

272

said that he had given us a gift…the gift of strength. He had a big set of weights in the corner of the room and told us to go prove it to ourselves. We did, and we were both shocked at how much we could lift. Whatever he gave us made both of us super strong. At first, he was very nice to us. He gave us a room where we could stay in the same building as the lab. He bought us pizza, brought us to his house to play video games, and taught us how to work out to make the most of our new abilities. As time went on though, we felt like something wasn't right. We told him we wanted to go home and that's when he got really mad. He said that if we left, he would hurt our family. We were scared to leave, but we knew that whatever he was planning to do wasn't right, so we escaped."

"Wow, what an incredible story," Shelley said, turning toward the camera, "and now, what you have all been waiting to see. Ethan and Ryan have agreed to demonstrate their claims of super strength live right here on our show."

Just as she was talking, a news van pulled up in the background. Shelley and the two boys stood from their chairs. Shelley, still facing the camera, continued.

"This is one of our remote news vans and, as you can see, it just pulled in behind us. No movie tricks or special effects here. This van weighs just over 10,000 pounds and, as you just saw, is fully functional."

Ethan walked to the front of the van while Ryan walked to the rear of the van. Each of them reached down to grab the bumper of the vehicle as Ethan started counting down from three. At the end of his countdown, both boys lifted, and the van rose completely off the ground. They held the van suspended in the air for about ten seconds before letting it down gently.

"Amazing," Shelley said staring into the camera, "back to you, Alyssa."

"Thank you, Shelley. Joining us now live from Washington, D.C. is Nolan Matthews, Director of the FBI. Good morning, and welcome to the show, Director Matthews."

"Good morning, Alyssa. I'm glad to be here."

"We've just heard and seen the incredible testimony of these brave boys. According to the official police statement taken when they were found, the man behind this is Tom Marshall, a former government agent. Can you give us any details on this suspect?"

"Not a lot, Alyssa. This case is still under investigation, and we have every possible resource actively working to find him and bring him in for questioning."

"Thank you, Director. Apparently, this man worked as some type of government agent. Can you tell us anything about his past, like who he worked for specifically?"

"Most of that is classified, but I can tell you that he certainly fits the profile of someone we would be interested in questioning in a case like this. He was a reclusive individual with no close friends or family to speak of."

"Thank you, Director," Alyssa said as she turned her full attention to the camera, "we'll share more details on this developing story as they become available."

Kyle pressed the button on the remote control to turn the television off and looked at Tom, who was still sipping his coffee.

"That was hurtful," Kyle said.

"Yes, it was," Tom replied.

"Do you think people believe them?" Kyle asked.

"They don't have any reason not to." Tom responded, lowering his cup.

"But it's not true," Kyle said.

"Unfortunately, most people don't care about truth. They care about what stirs their emotions. I'll give Jeff credit. As much as I hate it, this is a smart play on his part. If he can't persuade me, contain me, or control me, he can ruin me."

"They said they got strong with a shot. That's not even how it works though. Why would they say anything about a shot?"

"Well," Tom replied, "for starters, it makes them appear to be the victims as if they didn't have any control over what happened to them. I also suspect that Jeff doesn't want to reveal the truth about the restrainer chips. If everyone knows about the elite, his advantage is at risk."

"Do you think they're worried about getting caught?"

"No. After seeing what they have done and what they are willing to do, I don't think they're worried at all."

"Looks like Mr. George was right."

"Right about what?" Tom asked.

"The days of Noah."

"Maybe so."

"So, what do we do now?" Kyle asked.

"We need to leave the Atlanta area. There is just too much risk that one of us will be spotted here. Keeping everyone safe is my top priority."

"Where will we go?"

"I have a friend with some cabins in north Georgia. He said we can use them as long as we need."

"Is that the friend on the other end of the blue phone?" Kyle asked boldly.

"Yes," Tom said with a smirk, "yes, it is."

Kyle could tell that Tom was not interested in sharing any details about his friend beyond that conversation, so he dropped the subject.

"When do we leave?"

"At the end of the week," Tom replied, "There is one more item I need to take care of before we go."

Chapter 48

It had become my habit to consult with Robert when faced with a mystery I couldn't figure out. His advice was to pray and be still. I'm sure that is in the Bible somewhere, so I made a note to look it up later. His advice was difficult in our current environment. Everyone around me just had their world turned upside down. They were all looking to me for guidance. I had to plan out the next move, but there were too many unknowns. In addition to the pressure I felt, I was very skeptical that God would hand me the answers to all my questions just by praying.

After my long list of reasons not to take Robert's advice, I took a deep breath, found a quiet place, and yielded to his council. I didn't hear an audible voice, and there was no magical reference to a Bible verse that listed all the answers to my questions. What I did find was comfort. My mind cleared from all the fog of unanswered questions. My anxiety disappeared. I still felt responsible for this family, but I suddenly felt like I didn't need to lead them alone. As I write this, I realize that Robert was right. He usually is.

Admittedly, I was disappointed in myself. Having lived my whole life without close personal relationships, I feel like that void in my life has been filled now. As much as I cherish that, I let those emotions get in the way of sound judgement and put my new family at risk. I should have developed a plan before going after Riley. I should have recognized the traps set for me.

I questioned myself too. Am I really any better than Jeff? Whether I intended to or not, I put my friends at risk forcing, them to use their supernatural abilities to help me. Robert said the intention makes all the difference, but that doesn't stop me from beating myself up over it.

How could I have missed an elite? Based on what Jacob described, Cole was a formidable opponent, but he didn't even show up on my list. I checked the missing persons list and found a matching name—Cole Adams. Why did I just pass it over? I quickly put him at the top of my "danger" list, and then I pulled the record file on Cole. He must be one of Jeff's top recruits if he sent him up against Jacob.

He certainly fit the profile. Sixteen years old, raised by a single mom with no mention of a dad anywhere in the file. He had a history of mental health issues in recent years starting when he was twelve and extending as far as the records show. The record only showed his status until the time the department shut down. He was on and off anti-depressants since he was thirteen. His mom, Tori, was working two jobs just to maintain their survival and pay for his doctor visits and medicine.

Tori Adams had been a single mom most of Cole's life. I assumed she was the victim of some deadbeat guy who probably took advantage of her and then left her as soon as he found out she was pregnant. According to the records, Tori and Cole lived on the outskirts of Atlanta in a small rental house. She married a man named Larry Adams when Cole was three years old. Larry was so committed to Tori that he insisted on adopting Cole as his stepchild. Three years later, Cole's behavioral issues started to surface. It was too much for Larry to handle and he walked out on them both.

It was then I realized why I had dismissed him as a potential threat. He was listed as a Class 1 elite with heightened senses. That information didn't entirely match what Jacob described happened at the compound. The heightened senses would have given Cole an advantage when fighting Jacob in the dark, but only Class 3 elite had the strength that Jacob described. Is it possible that the record was incorrect? I had never encountered an incorrect record, but I supposed it was possible. The chip restrained each client's abilities, so we never had evidence of an incorrect record. Still, our risk mitigation classes were so important, this seemed like a huge miss. It was possible that Cole was a special case like Richard, but the record would have shown the higher Class.

I was convinced that there was something deeper going on. I was also perplexed by this anomaly. There was a passion inside of me to understand more. We all agreed to lay low for a while, but I had to figure out how and why Cole was so different than the record reflected. I committed to visit his last known home address in hopes of talking to his mom. Something in the pit of my stomach felt weird as I made the drive to the home address. Maybe I was afraid of being seen. What if someone was already a step ahead of me, and this was another trap? I really couldn't explain the feeling, and I wasn't sure what I would find.

I had rehearsed several conversation options in my head while driving over. None of them prepared me for what I was about to encounter. As I arrived, I checked the surroundings but didn't see anything out of the ordinary, so I felt like it was safe to proceed. I calmly walked to the front door and rang the doorbell.

The door opened, and I knew instantly that the woman who answered the door was Cole's mom. Our eyes locked onto each other. My mind immediately went blank, and I was overcome with shock. It was evident that she was feeling the same. I could feel the blood drain from my face. The emptiness of my mind was overcome by rapid-fire thoughts that I couldn't really express. As the thoughts were racing through my brain, I was trying to do the math in my head to verify my suspicions. *It's been so long. I can't believe it's her. What can I possibly say? If she is Cole's mom, then Cole must be...*

My thought process was interrupted by her words. She said the only thing she could think to say.

"Hello, Tom," she said, "it's been a long time."

"Hello, Victoria."

Tom Marshall Personal Log File BISA546
End of Record

Coming Next in the Series:

Remnant of the Elite

Made in the USA
Las Vegas, NV
19 November 2021